STAR WARS®

HEAD -TO- HEAD

TAG TEAMS

Pablo Hidalgo

SCHOLASTIC

New York · Toronto · London · Auckland · Sydney · Mexico City · New Delhi · Hong Kong

www.starwars.com

www.scholastic.com

Published by Scholastic Inc., 557 Broadway, New York, NY 10012;
Scholastic Canada Ltd., Markham, Ontario; Scholastic Australia
Pty. Ltd, Gosford NSW; Scholastic New Zealand Ltd., Greenmount,
Auckland; Scholastic UK, Coventry, Warwickshire

Produced by becker&mayer!
11120 NE 33rd Place, Suite 101
Bellevue, WA 98004
www.beckermayer.com

becker&mayer!
BOOK PRODUCERS

If you have questions or comments about this product, please visit www.
beckermayer/customerservice and click on Customer Service Request Form.

Edited by Ben Grossblatt
Designed by Sarah Baynes
Design assistance by Aileen Morrow
Image research by Zena Chew
Production management by Larry Weiner

Printed, manufactured, and assembled in Jefferson City, Missouri
First printing, January 2011

Special thanks to Carol Roeder, J. W. Rinzler, Troy Alders, and Leland Chee at LucasBooks

12 11 10 9 8 7 6 5 4 3 2 1   11 12 13 14 15/0

40

ISBN 978-0-545-31653-8

10198

HEAD-TO-HEAD
TAG TEAMS

Star Wars characters and creatures team up and battle it out like never before. For each battle, you'll see all the information—the stats, skills, and special details—you need to decide which team would be victorious! The last page features the experts' rulings on every battle.

THE TEAM-UPS

ANAKIN SKYWALKER & MACE WINDU VS. COUNT DOOKU & SUPREME CHANCELLOR PALPATINE

Picture it: The Jedi have seen through Chancellor Palpatine's deception. Anakin learns that the seemingly kind man was not his friend, but instead a Sith Lord in disguise! Shocked at this discovery, Skywalker and Windu speed to an abandoned warehouse on Coruscant, where the Sith Lords conspire.

BATTLEGROUND

Coruscant:
Dacho District,
"The Works"

ANAKIN SKYWALKER

Padawan with boundless confidence who often takes foolhardy risks

TEAM 1

MACE WINDU

Powerful, no-nonsense Jedi Master with a rigidly controlled fighting style

TEAM 1	ANAKIN SKYWALKER	MACE WINDU
Homeworld	Tatooine	Haruun Kal
Affiliation	Jedi	Jedi
Species	Human	Human
Height/Weight	1.85 meters/82 kilograms	1.88 meters/84 kilograms
Weapons	Lightsaber (blue blade)	Lightsaber (purple blade)
Special move	Lunge attack	Behind-the-back parry and strike

Intelligence 15
Strength 17
Agility 15
Damage 16
Control 17
Courage 20

THE SHOWDOWN

The impressionable Anakin is less able to put aside his surprise at discovering the deeply rooted Sith conspiracy than the steady Mace Windu. Dooku takes advantage of Anakin's distraction to release a torrent of lightning at the Jedi intruders. Once, Palpatine would have spared Anakin, but with his entire plot of galactic conquest threatened, the shadowy Sith Lord will destroy anyone who obstructs his path to absolute power. Can Anakin collect his bearings and work with Mace—a Jedi Master with whom he hasn't always seen eye-to-eye?

BATTLE BREAKDOWN
Comparative combat skills

OFFENSE DEFENSE

COUNT DOOKU
SUPREME CHANCELLOR PALPATINE
ANAKIN SKYWALKER
MACE WINDU

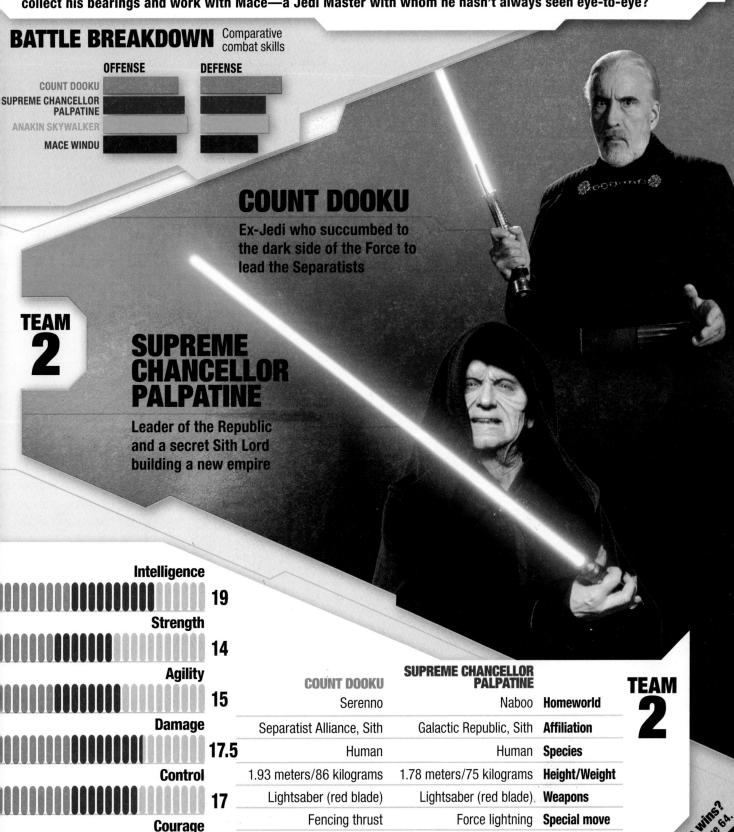

COUNT DOOKU
Ex-Jedi who succumbed to the dark side of the Force to lead the Separatists

TEAM 2

SUPREME CHANCELLOR PALPATINE
Leader of the Republic and a secret Sith Lord building a new empire

Intelligence
19

Strength
14

Agility
15

Damage
17.5

Control
17

Courage
13

	COUNT DOOKU	SUPREME CHANCELLOR PALPATINE	
	Serenno	Naboo	Homeworld
	Separatist Alliance, Sith	Galactic Republic, Sith	Affiliation
	Human	Human	Species
	1.93 meters/86 kilograms	1.78 meters/75 kilograms	Height/Weight
	Lightsaber (red blade)	Lightsaber (red blade)	Weapons
	Fencing thrust	Force lightning	Special move

TEAM 2

Who wins? See page 64.

LUKE SKYWALKER, DEWBACK & BIGGS DARKLIGHTER VS. GAMORREAN GUARD, GIRAN & JABBA'S RANCOR

A detour in the Tatooine wilderness can quickly turn deadly. Local boys Biggs and Luke ride a loyal dewback into the cooling shadows of Beggar's Canyon to escape the blazing suns overhead. There, they stumble across one of Jabba's beast-masters, Giran, taking his beloved rancor for a walk alongside a Gamorrean protector. The rancor's hungry howls soon echo off the canyon walls....

BATTLEGROUND
Tatooine:
Beggar's Canyon

DEWBACK
Herbivorous reptile commonly used as animal labor on Tatooine

BIGGS DARKLIGHTER
Academy cadet beginning to discover the true nature of the Empire

LUKE SKYWALKER
Daydreaming farm boy who longs for adventure and excitement

TEAM 1

	LUKE SKYWALKER	DEWBACK	BIGGS DARKLIGHTER
Homeworld	Tatooine	Tatooine	Tatooine
Affiliation	Lars moisture farm		The Academy
Species	Human		Human
Height/Weight	1.72 meters/ 77 kilograms	5.4 meters long/ 815 kilograms	1.83 meters/ 84 kilograms
Weapons	Hunting blaster rifle	Muscular build, heavy tail	Blaster pistol
Special move	Blaster rifle cross-parry	Tail-swat	Academy martial arts

TEAM 1

Intelligence	17
Strength	24.5
Agility	15
Damage	16
Control	19
Courage	21

6

THE SHOWDOWN

Biggs and Luke have heard tales of horrid beasts that Jabba keeps for his amusement, but this is their first encounter with such a nightmare. The dewback bucks off his two riders and panics, trying to scramble out of the gravelly canyon and escape the danger. The ravenous rancor eyes the most satisfying morsel amid a buffet of prey: the well-muscled dewback. Giran tries in vain to rein the rancor in, while the violent Gamorrean sees the humans as a chance to practice his axe skills.

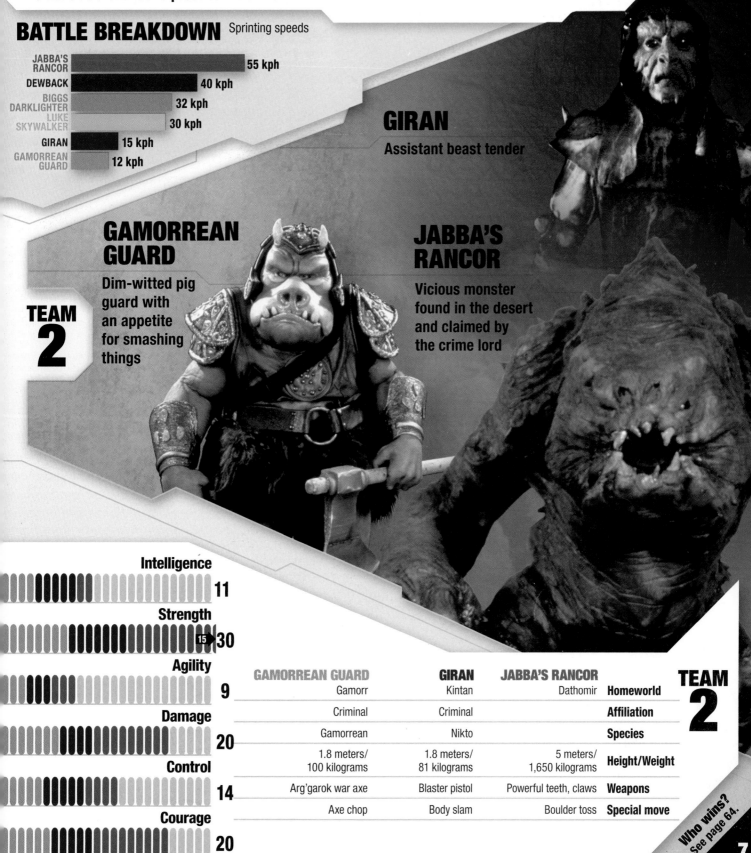

BATTLE BREAKDOWN — Sprinting speeds

JABBA'S RANCOR	55 kph
DEWBACK	40 kph
BIGGS DARKLIGHTER	32 kph
LUKE SKYWALKER	30 kph
GIRAN	15 kph
GAMORREAN GUARD	12 kph

GIRAN
Assistant beast tender

GAMORREAN GUARD
Dim-witted pig guard with an appetite for smashing things

TEAM 2

JABBA'S RANCOR
Vicious monster found in the desert and claimed by the crime lord

Intelligence **11**

Strength **15▶30**

Agility **9**

Damage **20**

Control **14**

Courage **20**

	GAMORREAN GUARD	GIRAN	JABBA'S RANCOR	
Homeworld	Gamorr	Kintan	Dathomir	
Affiliation	Criminal	Criminal		
Species	Gamorrean	Nikto		
Height/Weight	1.8 meters/ 100 kilograms	1.8 meters/ 81 kilograms	5 meters/ 1,650 kilograms	
Weapons	Arg'garok war axe	Blaster pistol	Powerful teeth, claws	
Special move	Axe chop	Body slam	Boulder toss	

TEAM 2

Who wins? See page 64.

7

SEBULBA, DUD BOLT & PIT DROID VS. YOUNG ANAKIN, KITSTER BANAI & WALD

Sticky-fingered Wald uses the bustle of the Podrace hangar as cover to steal a poorly guarded power charge for a Podracer. The burly Dud Bolt catches the thief, and Wald's loyal friends Anakin and Kitster come to his rescue. When Sebulba joins the fray, these childish high jinks suddenly turn very serious.

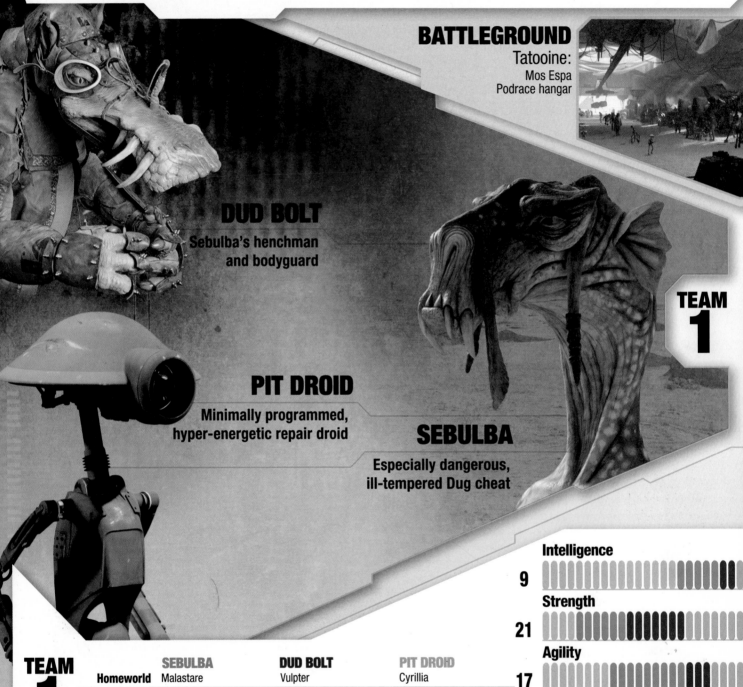

BATTLEGROUND
Tatooine:
Mos Espa
Podrace hangar

DUD BOLT
Sebulba's henchman and bodyguard

PIT DROID
Minimally programmed, hyper-energetic repair droid

SEBULBA
Especially dangerous, ill-tempered Dug cheat

TEAM 1

TEAM 1		SEBULBA	DUD BOLT	PIT DROID
	Homeworld	Malastare	Vulpter	Cyrillia
	Affiliation	Professional Podrace circuit	Professional Podrace circuit	Professional Podrace circuit
	Species	Dug	Vulptereen	Serv-O-Droid
	Height/Weight	1.12 meters/ 40 kilograms	0.94 meters/ 45 kilograms	1.19 meters/ 35 kilograms
	Weapons	None	Club	Air gun
	Special move	Combination punch/kick	Head-butt charge	Heave and throw

Intelligence
9

Strength
21

Agility
17

Damage
17

Control
17

Courage
14

THE SHOWDOWN

The nasty Sebulba thinks very little of slaves, so he hurls withering Huttese insults at the boys. Anakin and his pals hold their ground, but Skywalker's temper flares when his friends are threatened. The dull-minded Dud Bolt snorts and charges his way forward, but the youngsters are fast enough to slip past his rushing attack. The most unpredictable element in this bout is the pit droid. The frazzled mechanic has been ordered simply to "clean up this mess"—so the overly literal droid uses its surprisingly enormous strength to heave combatants into a nearby bin.

BATTLE BREAKDOWN — Comparative fighting experience

- DUD BOLT
- SEBULBA
- YOUNG ANAKIN
- WALD
- KITSTER BANAI
- PIT DROID

KITSTER BANAI

Anakin's best friend, also a slave, with dreams of serving a wealthy estate

YOUNG ANAKIN

Slave boy, expert mechanic, and amazing Podracer pilot

TEAM 2

WALD

Sneaky little Rodian with a knack for stirring up trouble

	Intelligence	**16**
	Strength	**11**
	Agility	**17**
	Damage	**10**
	Control	**17**
	Courage	**21**

	YOUNG ANAKIN	KITSTER BANAI	WALD	
Homeworld	Tatooine	Tatooine	Tatooine	
Affiliation	Slave	Slave	Slave	
Species	Human	Human	Rodian	
Height/Weight	1.35 meters/ 35 kilograms	1.24 meters/ 31 kilograms	0.86 meters/ 34 kilograms	
Weapons	None	Hydrospanner	Bag of marbles	
Special move	Low tackle	The "look behind you!" feint	Tumble-roll at enemy's feet	

TEAM 2

Who wins? See page 64.

DENGAR & GREEDO VS. HAN SOLO & NIEN NUNB

It's bounty hunters against smugglers as Greedo and Dengar team up against a pair of freighter-piloting rogues. Both professions require cunning and icy nerves, but while smugglers rely on clever tactics, bounty hunters are more likely to use their weapons to complete the job.

BATTLEGROUND
Tatooine:
Mos Eisley Spaceport

DENGAR
Cybernetically enhanced bounty hunter with a longstanding grudge against Solo

GREEDO
Secretive, impulsive (and smelly) bounty hunter

TEAM 1

	DENGAR	GREEDO
Homeworld	Corellia	Rodia
Affiliation	Bounty hunter	Bounty hunter
Species	Human (enhanced)	Rodian
Height/Weight	1.8 meters/95 kilograms	1.73 meters/74 kilograms
Weapons	Valken-38 blaster carbine	BlasTech DT-12 blaster pistol
Special move	Concussion grenade attack	"Shoot first" quick draw

Intelligence	11
Strength	12
Agility	9
Damage	14
Control	11
Courage	12

THE SHOWDOWN

The two smugglers, more than others in their line of work, know the value of loyalty. Never ones to let their guard down in a seedy starport, Han and Nien fight well together, watching each other's back when the laser blasts start flying. The bounty hunters are accustomed to working alone—and both want to be the one to claim the sizable price on Han's head. They have a difficult time coordinating their onslaught, but they have the edge when it comes to firepower.

BATTLE BREAKDOWN
How much each fighter adds to the battle

DENGAR
HAN SOLO
TEAM 2
TEAM 1
NIEN NUNB
GREEDO

NIEN NUNB
Good-natured smuggler and freedom fighter

HAN SOLO
Highly skilled pilot with a taste for adventure and profit

TEAM 2

		Intelligence
		12

Intelligence 12

Strength 11

Agility 12

Damage 12

Control 13

Courage 19

HAN SOLO	NIEN NUNB	
Corellia	Sullust	Homeworld
Smuggler, Rebel Alliance	Smuggler, Rebel Alliance	Affiliation
Human	Sullustan	Species
1.8 meters/80 kilograms	1.6 meters/68 kilograms	Height/Weight
Modified BlasTech DL-44 heavy blaster pistol	Model 434 blaster pistol	Weapons
Reckless charge	Starship auto-start (remote hidden in gloves)	Special move

TEAM 2

Who wins? See page 64.

ZAM WESELL, ACKLAY & NEXU VS. SUN FAC, VARACTYL & ORRAY

Nothing is more dangerous than a bored Geonosian noble. Archduke Poggle the Lesser demands exotic entertainment, and so his underlings shove an unlikely group of deadly combatants into the execution arena. Shapeshifter Zam Wesell is in it for a huge prize, while Sun Fac, a royal Geonosian, fights to retain his reputation and standing.

BATTLEGROUND
Geonosis:
Arena of Justice

ACKLAY
Ferocious, spike-limbed monster with a toothy maw

NEXU
Agile, razor-clawed, twin-tailed beast

ZAM WESELL
Shapeshifting bounty hunter confident in her abilities

TEAM 1

TEAM 1

	ZAM WESELL	ACKLAY	NEXU
Homeworld	Zolan	Vendaxa	Cholganna
Affiliation	Bounty hunter		
Species	Clawdite		
Height/Weight	1.68 meters (variable)/ 55 kilograms	3.05 meters/ 1,200 kilograms	4.51 meters (with tail)/ 225 kilograms
Weapons	KiSteer 1284 sniper rifle; KYD-21 blaster pistol	Sharp teeth, stabbing claws	Sharp teeth, claws, swiping tail
Special move	Changeling chokehold	Shaking bite	Fierce pounce

Intelligence
11

Strength
28 ◄6

Agility
23

Damage
22

Control
20

Courage
17

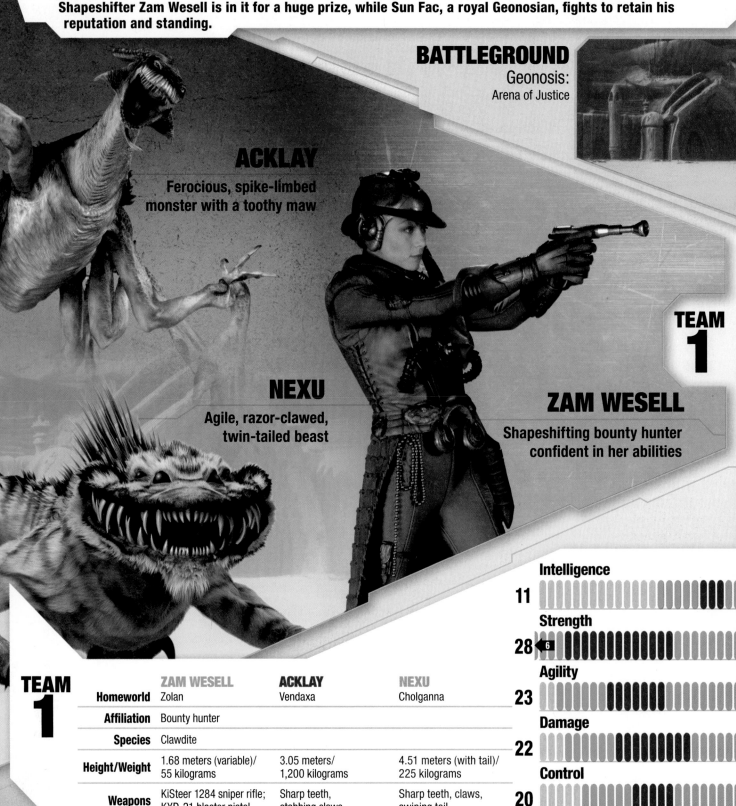

THE SHOWDOWN

Sun Fac's wings give him a great advantage, as the Geonosian can hover out of range of the nexu's and acklay's swipes. From this lofty height, he can lob sonic blasts at the beasts. Zam's shapeshifting abilities are of little help in the open battlefield of the arena, but her blaster rifle provides the longest-range attack of the combatants. The stabbing acklay is fast over short distances, but its spiked legs make it incapable of leaping like the nexu and the varactyl. Though not as spectacular as the more colorful creatures assembled, the orray is very loyal, and attacks at Sun Fac's command.

BATTLE BREAKDOWN

Who the Geonosians are betting on to be the last combatant standing

ZAM WESELL
SUN FAC
TEAM 2
VARACTYL
TEAM 1
ORRAY
ACLAY
NEXU

SUN FAC
Winged Geonosian aristocrat capable of cruelty

TEAM 2

VARACTYL
Feathered lizard with a sharp beak and impressive climbing ability

ORRAY
Simpleminded but loyal mount with a strong bite

	Intelligence	11
	Strength	24
	Agility	21
	Damage	16
	Control	16
	Courage	18

	SUN FAC	VARACTYL	ORRAY	
	Geonosis	Utapau	Geonosis	**Homeworld**
	Separatist Alliance			**Affiliation**
	Geonosian			**Species**
	1.71 meters/ 72 kilograms	15 meters/ 1,150 kilograms	3 meters/ 410 kilograms	**Height/Weight**
	GW sonic blaster cannon, electro-pike	Beak, spiked tail	Strong bite	**Weapons**
	Dive-bomb attack	Tail swipe	Head butt	**Special move**

TEAM 2

Who wins? See page 64.

BOBA FETT & GENERAL GRIEVOUS

 VS.

OBI-WAN KENOBI & CHEWBACCA

Through the Force come visions of other places, other times, and friends and foes from many paths. With meditation, a Jedi can conjure vivid dreams of conflicts that could never occur, like this imaginary clash amid the polished buildings on the swaying bridges of Cato Neimoidia.

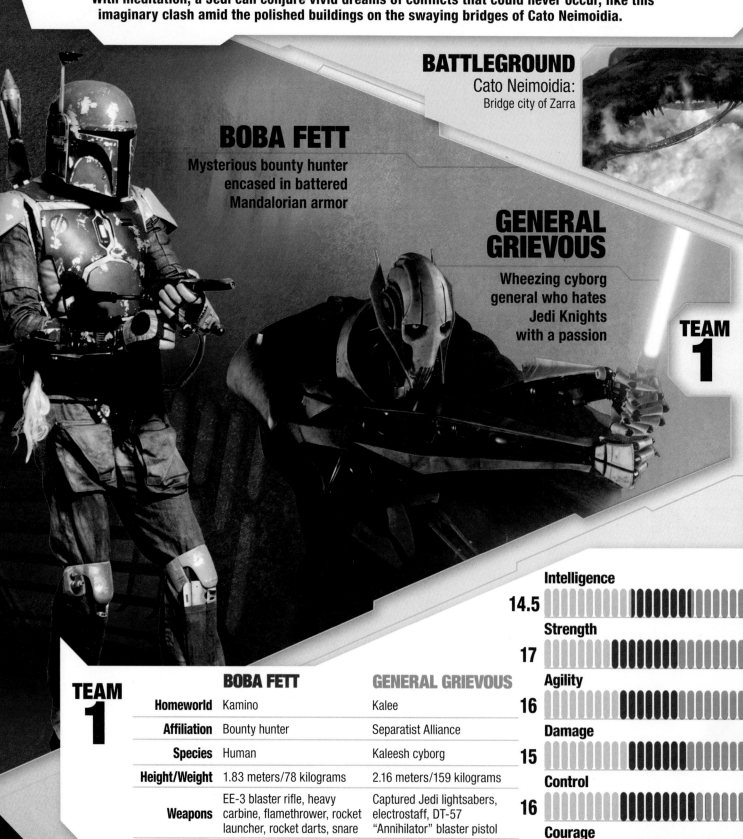

BATTLEGROUND
Cato Neimoidia: Bridge city of Zarra

BOBA FETT
Mysterious bounty hunter encased in battered Mandalorian armor

GENERAL GRIEVOUS
Wheezing cyborg general who hates Jedi Knights with a passion

TEAM 1

TEAM 1

	BOBA FETT	GENERAL GRIEVOUS
Homeworld	Kamino	Kalee
Affiliation	Bounty hunter	Separatist Alliance
Species	Human	Kaleesh cyborg
Height/Weight	1.83 meters/78 kilograms	2.16 meters/159 kilograms
Weapons	EE-3 blaster rifle, heavy carbine, flamethrower, rocket launcher, rocket darts, snare	Captured Jedi lightsabers, electrostaff, DT-57 "Annihilator" blaster pistol
Special move	Flamethrower attack	Four-arm whirlwind with lightsabers

Intelligence 14.5
Strength 17
Agility 16
Damage 15
Control 16
Courage 14

The gusty winds of Cato Neimoidia effectively ground Boba Fett, who won't risk losing control of his rocket pack. Grievous is so focused on his hatred of the Jedi that he mostly ignores Chewbacca, until the Wookiee closes in enough to tear a few of the general's arms from their sockets. But Grievous has limbs to spare, and when the fight gets too tight to use blasters and instead turns to fists and lightsabers, the outcome is anyone's guess.

BATTLE BREAKDOWN
How much each fighter adds to the battle

BOBA FETT

OBI-WAN KENOBI

TEAM 1

TEAM 2

CHEWBACCA

GENERAL GRIEVOUS

OBI-WAN KENOBI
A venerable Jedi Knight who prefers negotiation to combat

TEAM 2

CHEWBACCA
Wookiee warrior, expert mechanic, and loyal friend

Intelligence
14

Strength
17

Agility
12.5

Damage
15

Control
14

Courage
17

OBI-WAN KENOBI	CHEWBACCA		TEAM 2
Stewjon	Kashyyyk	**Homeworld**	
Jedi	Smuggler, Rebel Alliance	**Affiliation**	
Human	Wookiee	**Species**	
1.79 meters/81 kilograms	2.28 meters/112 kilograms	**Height/Weight**	
Lightsaber (blue blade)	Bowcaster	**Weapons**	
Sudden Force push	Arm-ripper pull	**Special move**	

Who wins? See page 64.

NUTE GUNRAY, RUNE HAAKO & FALUMPASET VS. JAR JAR BINKS, C-3PO & SIO BIBBLE

After another failed attempt to recapture Naboo, the Neimoidian leaders suffer the indignity of having to escape into the swamps atop a grumpy falumpaset. The two misplaced trade barons stumble upon a diplomatic tour of the wetlands undertaken by Jar Jar and Governor Bibble. As C-3PO would say, "Oh my!"

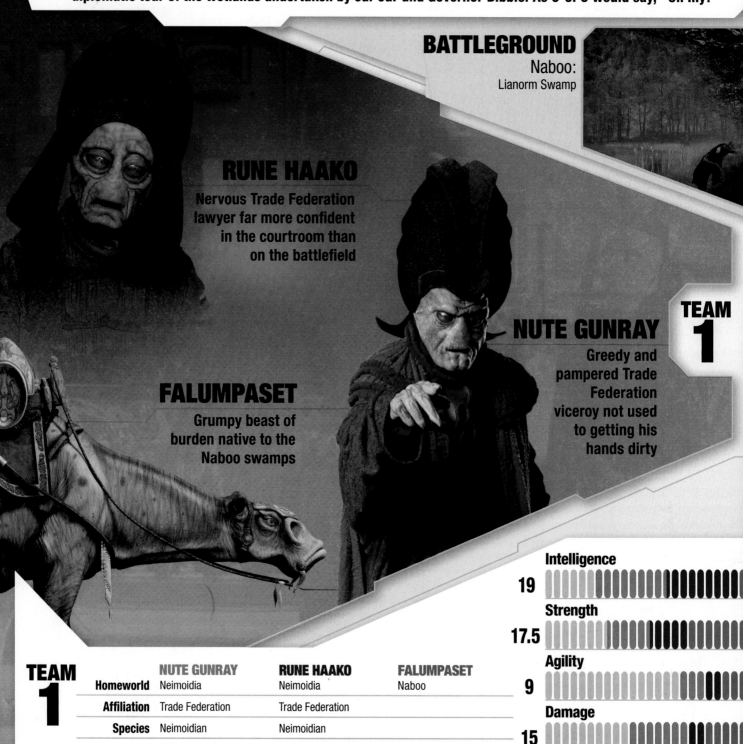

BATTLEGROUND
Naboo:
Lianorm Swamp

RUNE HAAKO
Nervous Trade Federation lawyer far more confident in the courtroom than on the battlefield

FALUMPASET
Grumpy beast of burden native to the Naboo swamps

NUTE GUNRAY
Greedy and pampered Trade Federation viceroy not used to getting his hands dirty

TEAM 1

TEAM 1		NUTE GUNRAY	RUNE HAAKO	FALUMPASET
	Homeworld	Neimoidia	Neimoidia	Naboo
	Affiliation	Trade Federation	Trade Federation	
	Species	Neimoidian	Neimoidian	
	Height/Weight	1.96 meters/ 90 kilograms	1.96 meters/ 89 kilograms	3 meters/ 400 kilograms
	Weapons	None	Poison-tipped knife	Well-muscled body
	Special move	Two-fisted wallop from behind	Stab-in-the-back	Squash

Intelligence
19

Strength
17.5

Agility
9

Damage
15

Control
12

Courage
14

THE SHOWDOWN

The Neimoidians despise conflict and would do anything to avoid imprisonment. After trying to bribe their way out of a fight—appeals to greed are wasted on the protocol droid, Jar Jar, and Bibble—Gunray and Haako take a deep breath and charge atop their beast, hoping the animal will know what to do. In an attempt to avoid the falumpaset, C-3PO trips amid the roots, while Jar Jar, rushing to break the droid's fall, topples over some vines. That leaves Sio the only surefooted one of the lot.

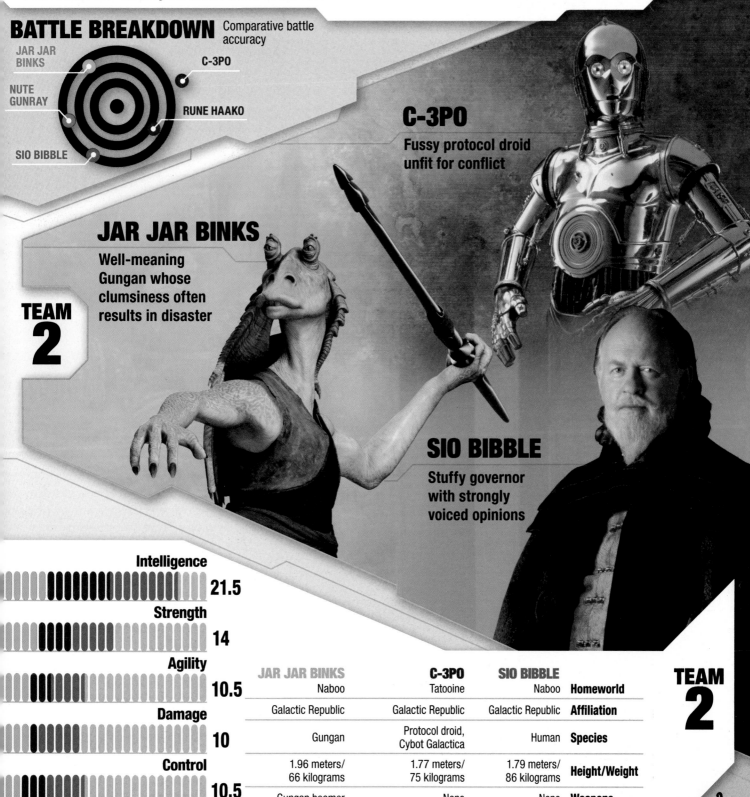

BATTLE BREAKDOWN
Comparative battle accuracy

JAR JAR BINKS

C-3PO

NUTE GUNRAY

RUNE HAAKO

SIO BIBBLE

C-3PO
Fussy protocol droid unfit for conflict

JAR JAR BINKS
Well-meaning Gungan whose clumsiness often results in disaster

TEAM 2

SIO BIBBLE
Stuffy governor with strongly voiced opinions

Intelligence
21.5

Strength
14

Agility
10.5

Damage
10

Control
10.5

Courage
15.5

	JAR JAR BINKS	C-3PO	SIO BIBBLE	
Homeworld	Naboo	Tatooine	Naboo	Homeworld
Affiliation	Galactic Republic	Galactic Republic	Galactic Republic	Affiliation
Species	Gungan	Protocol droid, Cybot Galactica	Human	Species
Height/Weight	1.96 meters/ 66 kilograms	1.77 meters/ 75 kilograms	1.79 meters/ 86 kilograms	Height/Weight
Weapons	Gungan boomer	None	None	Weapons
Special move	Tongue lash	Capable of begging for mercy in over 6 million forms of communication	Half-remembered self-defense training	Special move

TEAM 2

Who wins? See page 64.

GENERAL VEERS, IMPERIAL ROYAL GUARD & STORMTROOPER VS. MAGNAGUARD & IG-88

A mysterious, wealthy benefactor has hired IG-88 to assassinate the Emperor. The droid brings an IG-100 MagnaGuard for reinforcement. Together, they infiltrate the Emperor's spacious throne room only to discover that the target is absent. Not only that, but the droids have alerted a crack Imperial security team.

BATTLEGROUND
Death Star: Emperor's Throne Room

IMPERIAL ROYAL GUARD
Intensely trained elite guard of the Emperor

GENERAL VEERS
Effective and decorated Imperial officer who spearheaded the Hoth invasion

TEAM 1

STORMTROOPER
Loyal shock trooper of the Galactic Empire

TEAM 1

	GENERAL VEERS	IMPERIAL ROYAL GUARD	STORMTROOPER
Homeworld	Unknown	Unknown	Carida
Affiliation	Galactic Empire	Galactic Empire	Galactic Empire
Species	Human	Human	Human
Height/Weight	1.93 meters/ 82 kilograms	1.8 meters/ 80 kilograms	1.83 meters/ 80 kilograms
Weapons	E-11 blaster rifle	SoroSuub Controller FP force pike, heavy blaster pistol	E-11 blaster rifle, DLT-19 heavy blaster rifle
Special move	Troop rally and charge	Pike stab	Targeted strike

Intelligence 19

Strength 21.5

Agility 16.5

Damage 20

Control 20

Courage 25

THE SHOWDOWN

Protecting the sanctity of the Emperor's personal chambers is very strong motivation for the fiercely loyal Imperials. How does such inspiration compare to precision logic and programming? IG-88 is quick to realize that his objective cannot be reached, and switches to a secondary directive: escaping intact. His multiple weapons erupt in a hailstorm of destructive power, forcing the Imperials to seek what little cover there is. This allows the MagnaGuard to close the distance and engage the enemy one-on-one. Blaster bolts and explosive shrapnel ricochet off the gleaming surfaces in the throne room, missing the panoramic viewports by centimeters.

BATTLE BREAKDOWN
How much each fighter adds to the battle

STORMTROOPER
MAGNAGUARD
TEAM 2
IMPERIAL ROYAL GUARD
IG-88
GENERAL VEERS
TEAM 1

MAGNAGUARD
Precision-engineered bodyguard droid programmed for multiple forms of combat

TEAM 2

IG-88
Dangerously destructive, self-aware assassin droid

Intelligence **10**

Strength **17**

Agility **13**

Damage **17**

Control **15**

Courage **11**

MAGNAGUARD	IG-88	
Various	Holowan Laboratories	**Homeworld**
Separatist Alliance	Bounty hunter	**Affiliation**
IG-100 series bodyguard droid, Holowan Mechanicals	Assassin droid, Holowan Mechanicals	**Droid Type**
1.95 meters/ 123 kilograms	1.96 meters/ 140 kilograms	**Height/Weight**
Electrostaff, DT-57 "Annihilator" blaster pistol	Pulse cannon, riot gun, sonic stunner, thermal detonator	**Weapons**
Staff twirl	Sonic blast	**Special move**

TEAM 2

Who wins? See page 64.

19

PLO KOON, KI-ADI-MUNDI & AGEN KOLAR

VS.

AIWHA, SANDO AQUA MONSTER & COLO CLAW FISH

Kaminoan scientists have attempted to clone some of the most dangerous deepwater creatures. The horrors have escaped their habitats, and the snapping sea monsters threaten Tipoca City's stilt foundations. A Jedi team arrives in the churning oceans in a bid to corral the beasts.

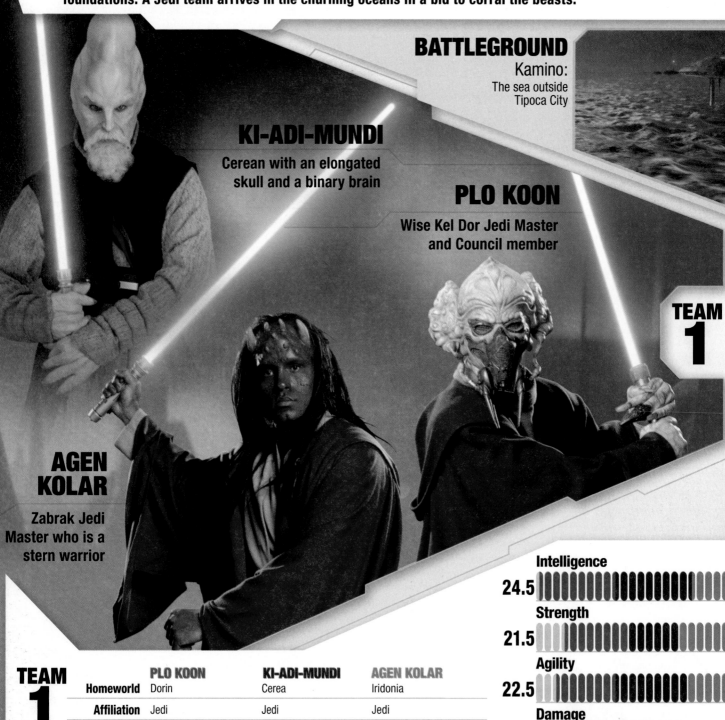

BATTLEGROUND

Kamino:
The sea outside
Tipoca City

KI-ADI-MUNDI

Cerean with an elongated skull and a binary brain

PLO KOON

Wise Kel Dor Jedi Master and Council member

TEAM 1

AGEN KOLAR

Zabrak Jedi Master who is a stern warrior

TEAM 1		PLO KOON	KI-ADI-MUNDI	AGEN KOLAR
	Homeworld	Dorin	Cerea	Iridonia
	Affiliation	Jedi	Jedi	Jedi
	Species	Kel Dor	Cerean	Zabrak
	Height/Weight	1.88 meters/ 80 kilograms	1.98 meters/ 82 kilograms	1.9 meters/ 82 kilograms
	Weapons	Lightsaber (blue blade)	Lightsaber (blue blade)	Lightsaber (blue blade)
	Special move	Armored talon slap	Glancing cut	Sudden Force push

Intelligence
24.5

Strength
21.5

Agility
22.5

Damage
21

Control
25.5

Courage
30

THE SHOWDOWN

Immense waves of water break against the supporting stilts of the city, and the Jedi must use their strength to keep from getting pitched into the restless seas. The creatures have sheer mass on their side, particularly the sando, which twists maddeningly. Though the Jedi could carve up their foes with lightsabers, they find taking the lives of such huge living things distasteful and against the principles of the Force. The poor creatures are the result of misguided science, after all, and their violent actions come from their distress, a fact the Jedi deeply respect.

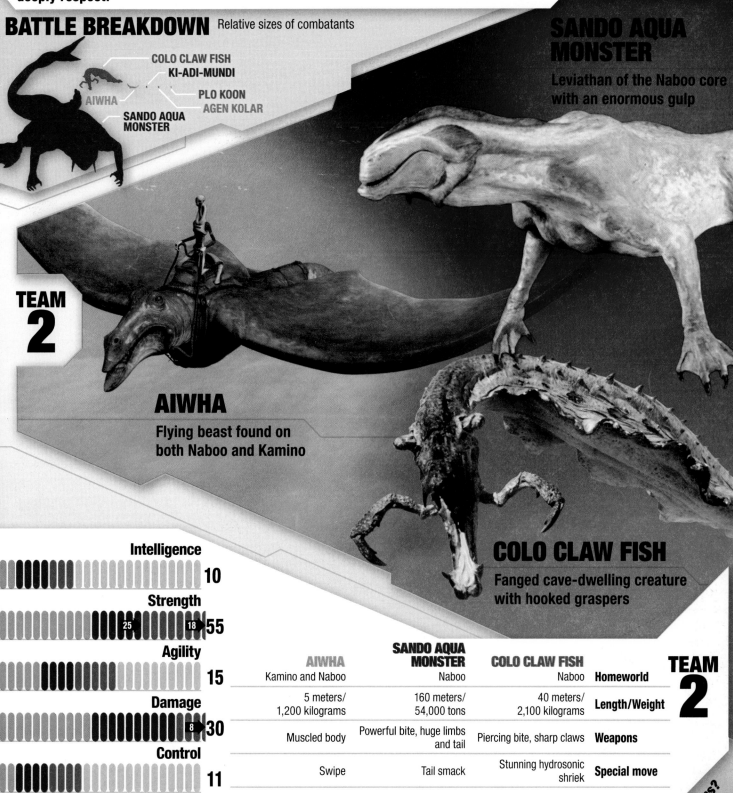

BATTLE BREAKDOWN Relative sizes of combatants

COLO CLAW FISH
KI-ADI-MUNDI
AIWHA
PLO KOON
AGEN KOLAR
SANDO AQUA MONSTER

SANDO AQUA MONSTER

Leviathan of the Naboo core with an enormous gulp

TEAM 2

AIWHA

Flying beast found on both Naboo and Kamino

COLO CLAW FISH

Fanged cave-dwelling creature with hooked graspers

Intelligence 10

Strength 25 18 →55

Agility 15

Damage 8 →30

Control 11

Courage 13

	AIWHA	SANDO AQUA MONSTER	COLO CLAW FISH		TEAM 2
Homeworld	Kamino and Naboo	Naboo	Naboo		
Length/Weight	5 meters/ 1,200 kilograms	160 meters/ 54,000 tons	40 meters/ 2,100 kilograms		
Weapons	Muscled body	Powerful bite, huge limbs and tail	Piercing bite, sharp claws		
Special move	Swipe	Tail smack	Stunning hydrosonic shriek		

Who wins? See page 64.

CAPTAIN TARPALS & KIT FISTO   VS. MUSTAFARIAN THIEF & LAVA FLEA

Captain Tarpals's investigations into stolen Naboo technology lead him to Mustafar. With Jedi Master Kit Fisto's help, he must stop the Mustafarian thief before he escapes atop a massive, armored lava flea. The Jedi and the Gungan are in close pursuit—will Mustafar's scorching landscape prove too great a challenge?

BATTLEGROUND
Mustafar:
Crusted-over lava plains

CAPTAIN TARPALS

Stalwart captain of the Gungan Grand Army forces

TEAM 1

KIT FISTO

Optimistic, tentacle-tressed aquatic Jedi Master

TEAM 1

	CAPTAIN TARPALS	KIT FISTO
Homeworld	Naboo	Glee Anselm
Affiliation	Gungan Grand Army	Jedi
Species	Gungan	Nautolan
Height/Weight	2.24 meters/82 kilograms	1.96 meters/87 kilograms
Weapons	Electropole, boomer-hurling cesta	Lightsaber (green blade)
Special move	Boomer throw	Force push

Intelligence
16

Strength
14.5

Agility
15

Damage
15.5

Control
13.5

Courage
18

THE SHOWDOWN

Mustafarian air contains not a drop of moisture, a fact that Tarpals and Fisto immediately feel in their lungs. The ovenlike conditions are draining, and Tarpals does not benefit from the healing Force abilities Kit has at his disposal. The Mustafarian thief immediately bolts—the speed and energy of his mount mean he expends no energy of his own. Kit and Tarpals can keep up for a time; Gungans are prodigious jumpers and Kit can Force leap, but before the fight even begins, it's an endurance contest. Can this acrobatic, aquatic duo go the distance across a searing obstacle course?

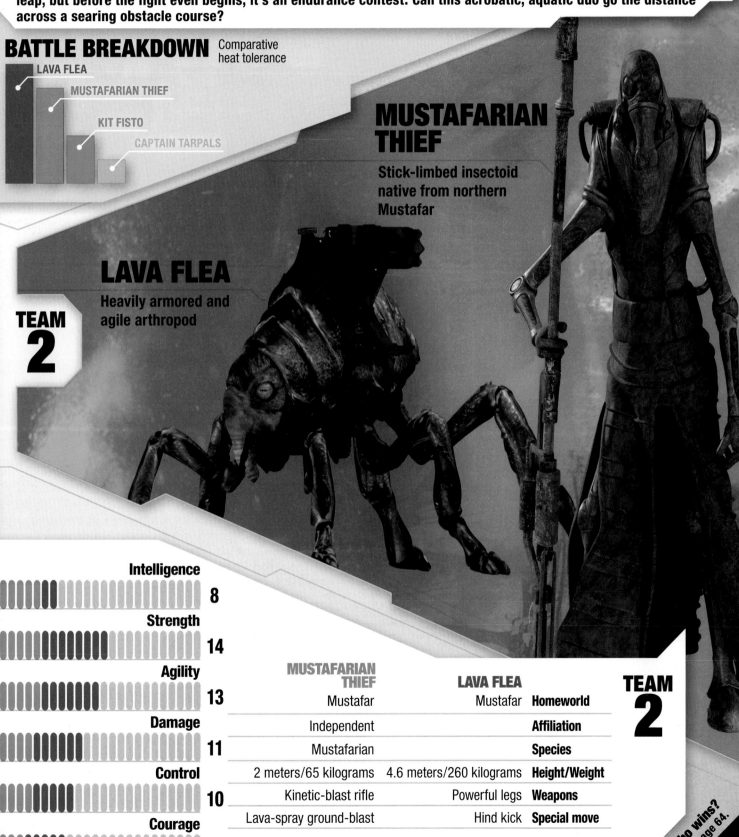

BATTLE BREAKDOWN
Comparative heat tolerance

- LAVA FLEA
- MUSTAFARIAN THIEF
- KIT FISTO
- CAPTAIN TARPALS

MUSTAFARIAN THIEF

Stick-limbed insectoid native from northern Mustafar

LAVA FLEA

Heavily armored and agile arthropod

TEAM 2

	Intelligence	**8**
	Strength	**14**
	Agility	**13**
	Damage	**11**
	Control	**10**
	Courage	**9**

MUSTAFARIAN THIEF	LAVA FLEA	
Mustafar	Mustafar	**Homeworld**
Independent		**Affiliation**
Mustafarian		**Species**
2 meters/65 kilograms	4.6 meters/260 kilograms	**Height/Weight**
Kinetic-blast rifle	Powerful legs	**Weapons**
Lava-spray ground-blast	Hind kick	**Special move**

TEAM 2

Who wins? See page 64.

LANDO CALRISSIAN, CLOUD CITY WING GUARD & LOBOT

VS.

DROIDEKA & UGNAUGHTS

Angry Ugnaught workers were caught sabotaging Cloud City's flotation systems. The Wing Guard police have cornered them in a carbon-freezing chamber, but the hog-men roll out heavy weaponry: a salvaged droideka. Administrator Lando Calrissian takes charge of the situation with his trusty computer-liaison officer, Lobot, and a city guard by his side.

BATTLEGROUND

Bespin:
Cloud City carbon-freezing chamber

CLOUD CITY WING GUARD

Loyal police officer serving and protecting Cloud City

LANDO CALRISSIAN

Dashing rogue who settled down to become administrator

TEAM 1

LOBOT

Tight-lipped cybernetically enhanced computer officer

TEAM 1

	LANDO CALRISSIAN	CLOUD CITY WING GUARD	LOBOT
Homeworld	Unknown	Bespin	Bespin
Affiliation	Rebel Alliance	Cloud City	Cloud City
Species	Human	Human	Human (enhanced)
Height/Weight	1.78 meters/ 79 kilograms	1.8 meters/ 80 kilograms	1.75 meters/ 79 kilograms
Weapons	Hold-out blaster	Relby-K23 blaster pistol	None
Special move	Bluff	Wide-beam stun blast	Telepathic computer interface

Intelligence
25 ||||||||||||||||||||||||||||||

Strength
18.5 ||||||||||||||||||||||||||||||

Agility
16.5 ||||||||||||||||||||||||||||||

Damage
15.5 ||||||||||||||||||||||||||||||

Control
24 ||||||||||||||||||||||||||||||

Courage
23.5 ||||||||||||||||||||||||||||||

THE SHOWDOWN

Lando prefers talking to shooting; he tries to use his authority as administrator to persuade the Ugnaughts to stand down, but they're too dedicated to their cause. The hog-men roll out their reprogrammed droideka. The machine is immune to any negotiation and pumps volleys of laser blasts at the Cloud City team. Lobot is strangely immobile, telepathically linking to the computer network controlling the room. The carbon-freezing chamber suddenly comes to life with a mix of light, noise, and steam, buying Lando's team a chance to regroup.

BATTLE BREAKDOWN

How much each fighter adds to the battle

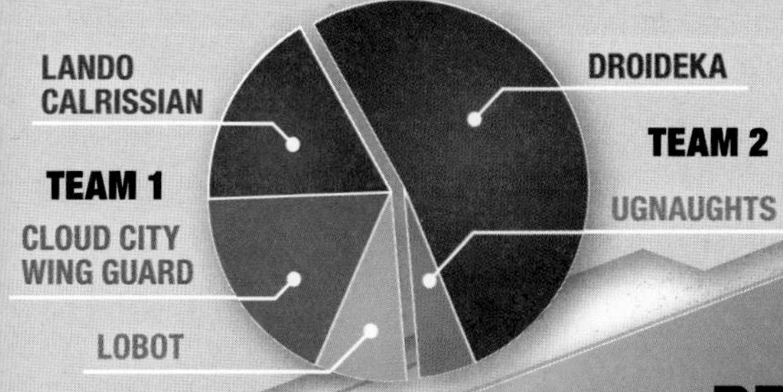

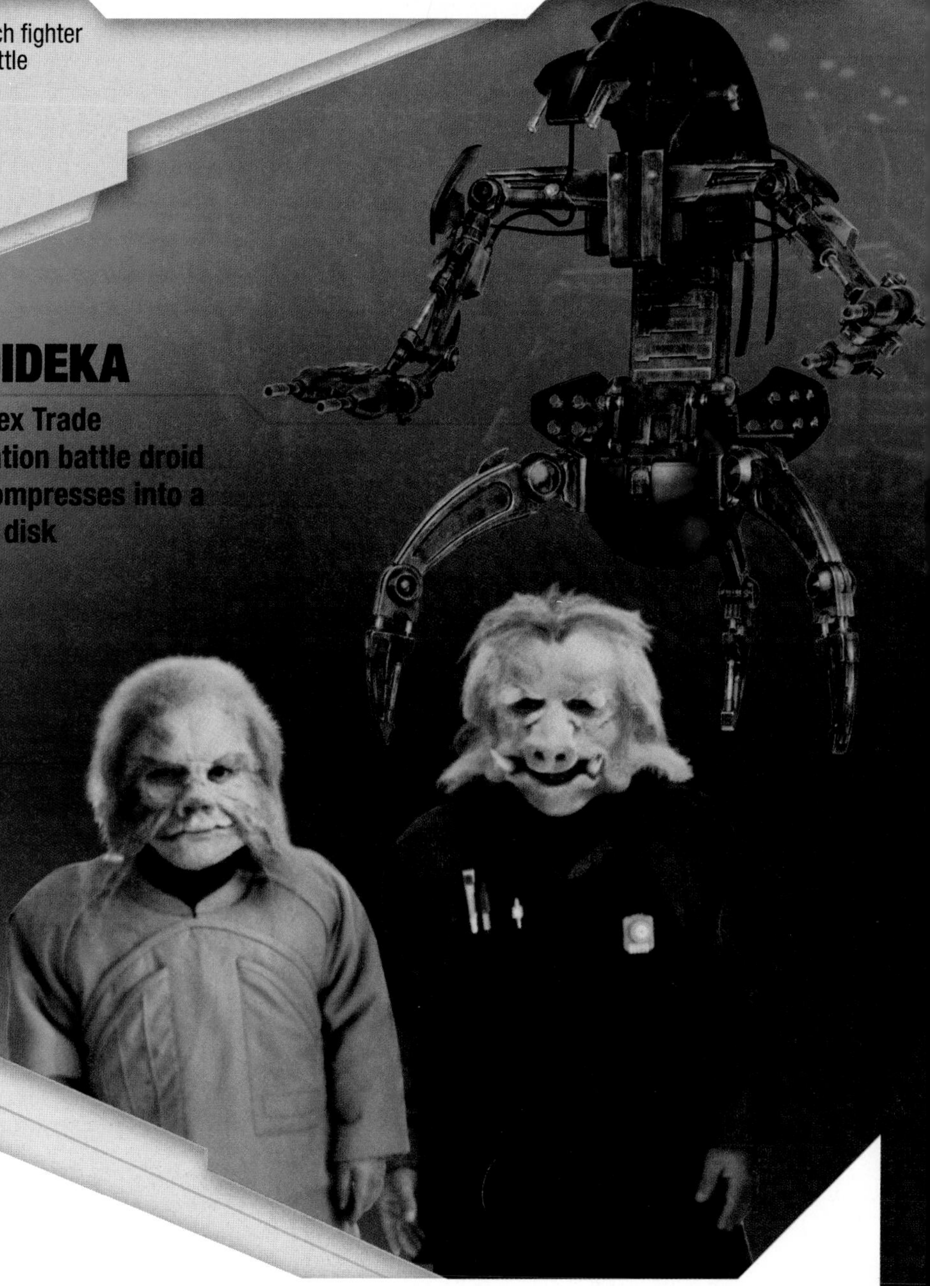

DROIDEKA

Complex Trade Federation battle droid that compresses into a rolling disk

TEAM 2

UGNAUGHTS

Fed-up laborers who know the inner workings of Cloud City

Intelligence 9

Strength 13.5

Agility 10

Damage 14

Control 13

Courage 12

TEAM 2

DROIDEKA	UGNAUGHTS	
Colla IV	Gentes	**Homeworld**
Separatist Alliance (reprogrammed)	Cloud City	**Affiliation**
Destroyer droid, Colicoid Creation Nest	Ugnaught	**Species**
1.83 meters/ 75 kilograms	1.1 meters/ 43 kilograms	**Height/Weight**
Two twin laser cannons	Hydrospanner, cutting torch	**Weapons**
Tumble charge	Carbonite chamber activation	**Special move**

Who wins? See page 64.

WEDGE ANTILLES & JEK PORKINS VS. CAPTAIN PIETT & TIE FIGHTER PILOT

How well do some of the galaxy's best pilots fare when they're not in their starships? A would-be diplomatic meeting in a Star Destroyer hangar is cut short by fiery tempers when a loose-lipped Imperial pilot insults Princess Leia. The gloves and helmets come flying off!

BATTLEGROUND
Star Destroyer *Accuser*:
Hangar bay

WEDGE ANTILLES
Longtime Rebel pilot

JEK PORKINS
Stout pilot who can be counted on for protection in a pinch

TEAM 1

	WEDGE ANTILLES	JEK PORKINS
Homeworld	Corellia	Bestine IV
Affiliation	Rebel Alliance	Rebel Alliance
Species	Human	Human
Height/Weight	1.7 meters/77 kilograms	1.78 meters/110 kilograms
Weapons	Blaster pistol	Heavy blaster pistol
Special move	Corellian haymaker punch	Belly slam

TEAM 1

Intelligence 13.5
Strength 12
Agility 9
Damage 12
Control 15
Courage 19

26

THE SHOWDOWN

Porkins doesn't take insults lightly. Personal ones, he can shrug off, but a surly Imperial pilot besmirching the reputations of the Rebel Alliance and Princess Leia Organa? Because she's not here to defend herself, Porkins takes matters into his own hands and tries to shut the pilot's mouth with his beefy fist. At first, Wedge holds his wingmate back, but when the Imperial keeps egging on the Rebels, Wedge joins in. Piett tries to maintain some decorum, but he, too, is pulled into fisticuffs.

BATTLE BREAKDOWN
Comparative leadership abilities of combatants

CAPTAIN PIETT
WEDGE ANTILLES
JEK PORKINS
TIE FIGHTER PILOT

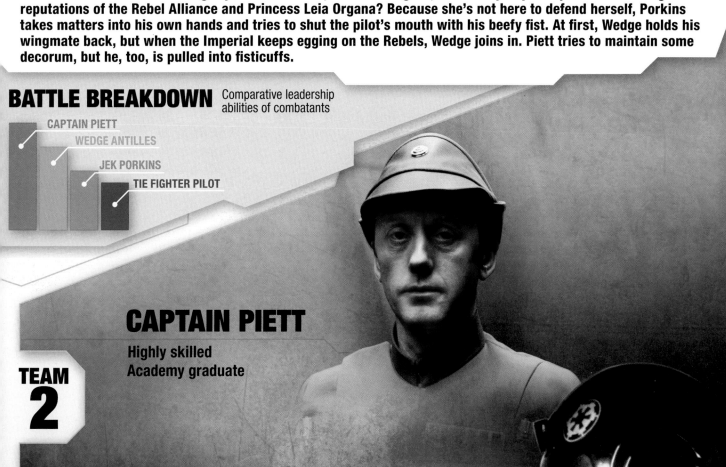

CAPTAIN PIETT

Highly skilled
Academy graduate

TEAM 2

TIE FIGHTER PILOT

Very capable pilot of the
Imperial Starfleet service

TEAM 2

Intelligence
14

Strength
11

Agility
10

Damage
10

Control
13

Courage
15

	CAPTAIN PIETT	TIE FIGHTER PILOT	
	Axxila	Unknown	**Homeworld**
	Galactic Empire	Galactic Empire	**Affiliation**
	Human	Human	**Species**
	1.65 meters/70 kilograms	1.8 meters/79 kilograms	**Height/Weight**
	Blaster pistol	Blaster pistols	**Weapons**
	Academy martial arts	Academy martial arts	**Special move**

Who wins?
See page 64.

OLD BEN KENOBI & RONTO VS. DICE IBEGON LAK SIVRAK & HEM DAZON

On a supply trip into Mos Eisley on a rented ronto, Ben Kenobi witnesses an altercation spill into the desert streets. Three Mos Eisley Cantina patrons—Dice Ibegon, Lak Sivrak, and Hem Dazon—were embroiled in a heated argument made hotter by the scorching Tatooine suns. Kenobi good-naturedly tries to settle the dispute, but the enraged aliens target him instead!

BATTLEGROUND
Tatooine:
Mos Eisley streets

OLD BEN KENOBI
Old desert hermit thought to be crazy by the locals

RONTO
Obedient saurian pack animal native to Tatooine

TEAM 1

	OLD BEN KENOBI	RONTO
Homeworld	Stewjon	Tatooine
Affiliation	Jedi	
Species	Human	
Height/Weight	1.75 meters/80 kilograms	4.25 meters/1,675 kilograms
Weapons	Lightsaber	Heavy feet
Special move	Jedi mind trck	Flatten

TEAM 1

Intelligence	12.5
Strength	22
Agility	9
Damage	16
Control	11
Courage	14

THE SHOWDOWN

Hem Dazon is the most ill-tempered of the aliens—a side effect of his salt addiction. Salt consumption affects his aim, as his talons tremble when he holds his blaster pistol. Still, the ronto is a large target. Lak Sivrak and Dice Ibegon are more even-keeled. Though Kenobi keeps his lightsaber handy, he is hesitant to use it, seeing as Jedi are not a welcome sight in these Imperial times.

BATTLE BREAKDOWN
Optimum striking ranges

LAK SIVRAK	15 meters
HEM DAZON	15 meters
DICE IBEGON	12 meters
RONTO	4 meters
OLD BEN KENOBI	3 meters

LAK SIVRAK
Former Imperial scout who now sympathizes with the Rebel Alliance

DICE IBEGON
Serpentine alien who can see glimpses of the future

HEM DAZON
Arconan Cantina patron addicted to salt, a substance unhealthy to his species

TEAM 2

Intelligence	19
Strength	19
Agility	19
Damage	24
Control	19
Courage	18

DICE IBEGON	LAK SIVRAK	HEM DAZON	
Florn	Uvena Prime	Cona	**Homeworld**
Rebel-leaning	Rebel-leaning	None	**Affiliation**
Lamproid	Shistavanen	Arcona	**Species**
1.3 meters/45 kilograms	1.82 meters/81 kilograms	1.65 meters/72 kilograms	**Height/Weight**
Poison stinger	Blaster rifle	Blaster pistol	**Weapons**
Force-confusion	Clamping bite	Backhanded claw-swipe	**Special move**

TEAM 2

Who wins? See page 64.

TARFFUL & MERUMERU VS. TANK DROID & DWARF SPIDER DROID

The Clone Wars explode through the formerly tranquil lagoons of Kashyyyk, the forest home of the Wookiees. The local forces—valiant warriors of great strength and even greater heart—gather to repel the relentless droid invaders. Wookiees swing into the fray on thick vines, landing in the thick of a droid beach landing.

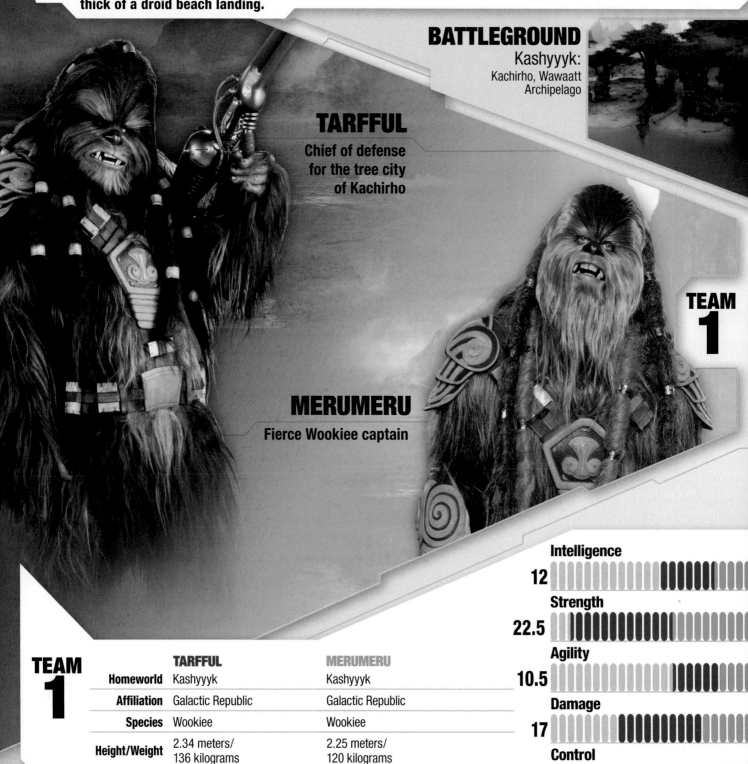

BATTLEGROUND
Kashyyyk: Kachirho, Wawaatt Archipelago

TARFFUL
Chief of defense for the tree city of Kachirho

MERUMERU
Fierce Wookiee captain

TEAM 1

TEAM 1		TARFFUL	MERUMERU
	Homeworld	Kashyyyk	Kashyyyk
	Affiliation	Galactic Republic	Galactic Republic
	Species	Wookiee	Wookiee
	Height/Weight	2.34 meters/ 136 kilograms	2.25 meters/ 120 kilograms
	Weapons	Bowcaster, Wookiee long-gun	Battle-staff, anti-vehicle mine, bowcaster
	Special move	Two-fisted downward smash	Affixing adhesive explosives

Intelligence 12

Strength 22.5

Agility 10.5

Damage 17

Control 14.5

Courage 16

30

THE SHOWDOWN

Jets of water spray from the tank droid's trio of treads as they cut through the shallow lagoon toward the well defended beachfront. The droid's frontal armor deflects and absorbs most of the incoming bowcaster bolts fired by the Wookiees, but if Tarfful and Merumeru can scramble up the boles of a massive nearby wroshyr tree, they can fire at the more exposed tail section. The dwarf spider droid, though, provides covering fire with its highly mobile and accurate main blaster cannon.

BATTLE BREAKDOWN

How much each fighter adds to the battle

- TANK DROID
- TARRFUL
- TEAM 2
- DWARF SPIDER DROID
- TEAM 1
- MERUMERU

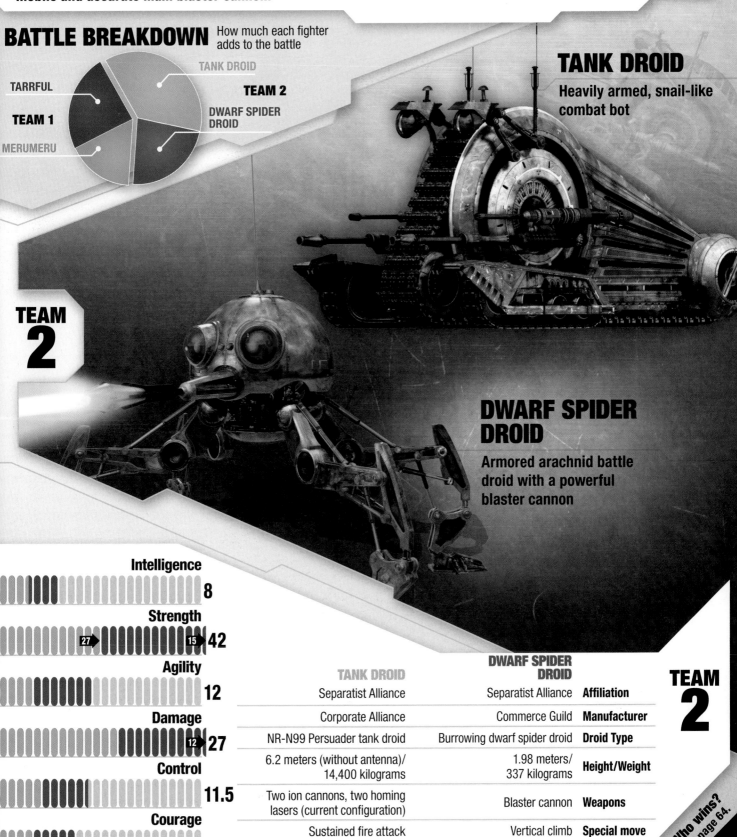

TANK DROID

Heavily armed, snail-like combat bot

TEAM 2

DWARF SPIDER DROID

Armored arachnid battle droid with a powerful blaster cannon

Intelligence 8

Strength 27 15 42

Agility 12

Damage 12 27

Control 11.5

Courage 10

	TANK DROID	DWARF SPIDER DROID	
	Separatist Alliance	Separatist Alliance	**Affiliation**
	Corporate Alliance	Commerce Guild	**Manufacturer**
	NR-N99 Persuader tank droid	Burrowing dwarf spider droid	**Droid Type**
	6.2 meters (without antenna)/ 14,400 kilograms	1.98 meters/ 337 kilograms	**Height/Weight**
	Two ion cannons, two homing lasers (current configuration)	Blaster cannon	**Weapons**
	Sustained fire attack	Vertical climb	**Special move**

TEAM 2

Who wins? See page 64.

31

COLEMAN TREBOR & ADI GALLIA VS. 4-LOM & AURRA SING

Jedi Masters Coleman Trebor and Adi Gallia have tracked bounty hunter Aurra Sing to the marshlands of Saleucami, but discover that she is not alone. Her hunting assignments have netted her a new partner: the reprogrammed protocol droid, 4-LOM. This insect-eyed automaton is interested in testing its calculations of the odds of defeating a Jedi Knight.

BATTLEGROUND
Saleucami:
Wetlands

COLEMAN TREBOR

Diplomatic, yet powerfully built, amphibious Jedi Master

TEAM 1

ADI GALLIA

Seemingly ageless Jedi with infallible intuition

TEAM 1

	COLEMAN TREBOR	ADI GALLIA
Homeworld	Sembla	Coruscant
Affiliation	Jedi	Jedi
Species	Vurk	Tholothian
Height/Weight	2.13 meters/90 kilograms	1.84 meters/50 kilograms
Weapons	Lightsaber (green blade)	Lightsaber (blue blade)
Special move	Blast reflection	Sudden Force push

Intelligence
15.5

Strength
13.5

Agility
17

Damage
13

Control
13

Courage
17

THE SHOWDOWN

As the battle erupts, 4-LOM immediately begins broadcasting a piercing electronic wail—something Aurra Sing is prepared for with ear protection. The Jedi are momentarily set back, and Coleman dives into a nearby lagoon to escape the sonic bombardment. When he recovers his senses and is ready to engage the hunters, he leaps from the water. Adi Gallia frantically deflects the incoming fire from Aurra Sing's twin blasters as she tries to regain the upper hand. Can the Jedi concentrate long enough to use the Force to best their enemies?

BATTLE BREAKDOWN

4-LOM's pre-battle calculations of each fighter's contribution

- COLEMAN TREBOR
- 4-LOM
- TEAM 2
- AURRA SING
- TEAM 1
- ADI GALLIA

4-LOM

TEAM 2

Older-model protocol droid that altered its own programming to become a hunter

AURRA SING

Gunslinging bounty hunter who despises Jedi

Intelligence		15
Strength		11.5
Agility		10
Damage		14
Control		14
Courage		12

4-LOM	AURRA SING	
Unknown	Nar Shaddaa	**Homeworld**
Bounty hunter	Bounty hunter	**Affiliation**
LOM protocol droid (reprogrammed), Industrial Automaton	Human hybrid	**Species**
1.6 meters/75 kilograms	1.74 meters/56 kilograms	**Height/Weight**
DLT-19 blaster rifle, concussion rifle, stun-gas blower	Czerka Adventurer sniper rifle, paired blaster pistols	**Weapons**
Ear-splitting sonic blast	Clawed swipe	**Special move**

TEAM 2

Who wins? See page 64.

PRINCESS LEIA & WICKET W. WARRICK VS. A DOZEN BUZZ DROIDS

In the aftermath of the second Death Star's destruction, Princess Leia and Wicket poke through the wreckage of the shield generator complex on Endor's forest moon. In one densely tangled nest of charred girders and shattered walls, they uncover a dozen chattering, maniacal buzz droids, programmed by scavengers to cut up and salvage the ruins.

BATTLEGROUND
Endor:
Forest moon

PRINCESS LEIA

Former Imperial Senator turned Rebel leader with an attunement to the Force

TEAM 1

WICKET W. WARRICK

Inquisitive Ewok scout who was the first to befriend the Rebels

TEAM 1

	PRINCESS LEIA	WICKET W. WARRICK
Homeworld	Alderaan	Forest moon of Endor
Affiliation	Rebel Alliance	Rebel Alliance
Species	Human	Ewok
Height/Weight	1.5 meters/49 kilograms	0.8 meters/20 kilograms
Weapons	Drearian Defender sporting blaster	Spear, sling
Special move	Fast draw	Vine swing-attack

Intelligence 14

Strength 11

Agility 9.5

Damage 8

Control 12.5

Courage 20

THE SHOWDOWN

The gang of buzz droids emerges from sooty corners, their red eyes flashing in the blackened wreckage of the bunker. The staccato clacking of their spiky feet warns Leia and Wicket of impending danger. Leia draws her blaster. Wicket readies his spear. Instinctively, they huddle back-to-back, though Leia towers over the brave Ewok. She fires first, shattering one of the buzz droids, which prompts the rest to charge in a leaping swarm. Wicket swats one out of the air, but it quickly rights itself and continues crawling forward. The buzz droids are relentless, but Leia and Wicket don't give up easily either.

BATTLE BREAKDOWN — Optimum weapon ranges

PRINCESS LEIA	15 meters
WICKET W. WARRICK	1.5 meters
BUZZ DROIDS	1 meter

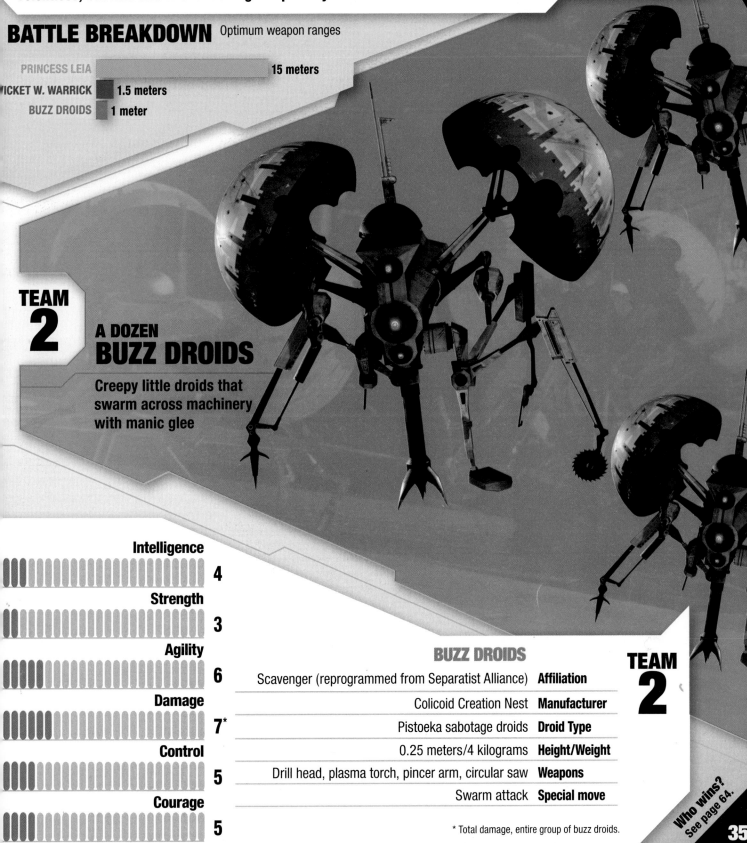

TEAM 2

A DOZEN BUZZ DROIDS

Creepy little droids that swarm across machinery with manic glee

Intelligence 4

Strength 3

Agility 6

Damage 7*

Control 5

Courage 5

BUZZ DROIDS

Scavenger (reprogrammed from Separatist Alliance)	**Affiliation**
Colicoid Creation Nest	**Manufacturer**
Pistoeka sabotage droids	**Droid Type**
0.25 meters/4 kilograms	**Height/Weight**
Drill head, plasma torch, pincer arm, circular saw	**Weapons**
Swarm attack	**Special move**

TEAM 2

* Total damage, entire group of buzz droids.

Who wins? See page 64.

JABBA THE HUTT, BUBO & POTE SNITKIN VS. BANTHA, TUSKEN CHIEF & TUSKEN RAIDER

To avoid an incoming dust storm, pilot Pote Snitkin has steered Jabba's sail barge into the twisting canyons of the Jundland Wastes. The vehicle's repulsorlift generator malfunctions when it scrapes against a sacred Tusken Raider cairn, stranding the vehicle in the midst of angry Sand People territory.

BATTLEGROUND
Tatooine:
Jundland Wastes

BUBO
Strange Frog-dog alien who is secretly intelligent

POTE SNITKIN
Jabba's thick-skinned chief vehicle operator

JABBA THE HUTT
Corpulent and corrupt leader of the Hutt criminal families

TEAM 1

TEAM 1	JABBA THE HUTT	BUBO	POTE SNITKIN
Homeworld	Nal Hutta	Tatooine	Agriworld-2079
Affiliation	Criminal	Criminal	Criminal
Species	Hutt	Frog-dog	Skrilling
Height/Weight	1.75 meters/ 1,358 kilograms	0.5 meters/ 35 kilograms	1.95 meters/ 90 kilograms
Weapons	None	Sharp teeth, hidden thermal detonator	Vibro-axe
Special move	Crushing roll	Bite and shake	Biological acid spray

Intelligence 18

Strength 23.5

Agility 10

Damage 16.5

Control 13

Courage 18

THE SHOWDOWN

The whooping, howling Tuskens descend from the upper canyons, firing their rifles at the barge. Though their blasts are recklessly scattered across the hull, one does pierce the fuel chamber, prompting an evacuation of the vehicle. Unable to use the barge as shelter, Jabba and his underlings are forced to fight. The fierce Tuskens charge the three most visible targets: the bloblike Jabba, the barking Bubo, and the burly Pote Snitkin. The bantha prevents any from escaping.

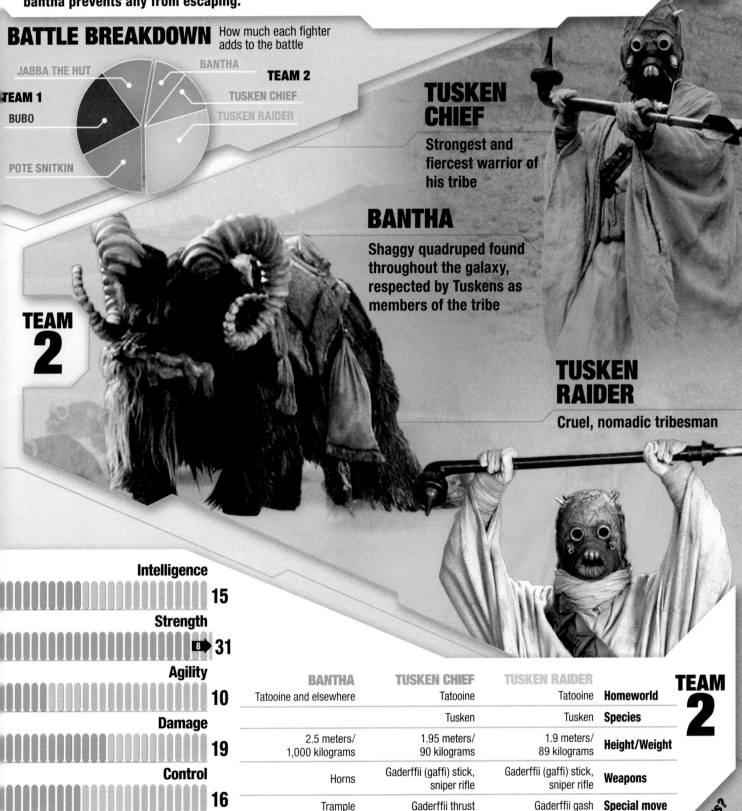

BATTLE BREAKDOWN
How much each fighter adds to the battle

- JABBA THE HUT
- TEAM 1
- BUBO
- POTE SNITKIN
- BANTHA
- TEAM 2
- TUSKEN CHIEF
- TUSKEN RAIDER

TUSKEN CHIEF
Strongest and fiercest warrior of his tribe

BANTHA
Shaggy quadruped found throughout the galaxy, respected by Tuskens as members of the tribe

TUSKEN RAIDER
Cruel, nomadic tribesman

TEAM 2

Intelligence **15**

Strength **8 ➤ 31**

Agility **10**

Damage **19**

Control **16**

Courage **18**

	BANTHA	TUSKEN CHIEF	TUSKEN RAIDER	
Homeworld	Tatooine and elsewhere	Tatooine	Tatooine	
Species		Tusken	Tusken	
Height/Weight	2.5 meters/ 1,000 kilograms	1.95 meters/ 90 kilograms	1.9 meters/ 89 kilograms	
Weapons	Horns	Gaderffii (gaffi) stick, sniper rifle	Gaderffii (gaffi) stick, sniper rifle	
Special move	Trample	Gaderffii thrust	Gaderffii gash	

TEAM **2**

Who wins? See page 64.

A Naboo diplomatic mission to Tatooine is a tempting opportunity for mercenaries and hunters looking to profit from the hefty price on Padmé Amidala's head. The Naboo star yacht is shot down and lands hard in the desert sands, skidding to a halt over the lip of the Great Pit of Carkoon.

BATTLEGROUND
Tatooine:
Pit of Carkoon

SABÉ
Handmaiden to Queen Amidala

CAPTAIN TYPHO
Battlefield veteran and Amidala's sworn protector

PADMÉ AMIDALA
Once a Queen, then a Senator, then mother to Luke Skywalker and Princess Leia

TEAM 1

	PADMÉ AMIDALA	SABÉ	CAPTAIN TYPHO
Homeworld	Naboo	Naboo	Naboo
Affiliation	Galactic Republic	Galactic Republic	Galactic Republic
Species	Human	Human	Human
Height/Weight	1.65 meters/ 45 kilograms	1.65 meters/ 45 kilograms	1.85 meters/ 85 kilograms
Weapons	ELG-3A royal pistol	ELG-3A royal pistol	Naboo blaster pistol
Special move	Swinging kick	Disarm	Ascension cable grapple

TEAM 1

Intelligence
23

Strength
18

Agility
17.5

Damage
14

Control
20.5

Courage
29

THE SHOWDOWN

The bounty on Amidala stipulates that proof of her elimination must be brought in. This requires the hunters to get in close, because a distant shot might send the Senator tumbling into the waiting Sarlacc. This is the way Dannik, Amanaman, and Myo prefer to battle—face-to-face. Myo's ability to heal wounds and regrow organs makes him the most fearless, and he rushes into combat. Dannik senses great potential in Padmé, something that stokes his hungry vampire-like appetite. Sabé and Typho are determined to protect the Senator at all costs.

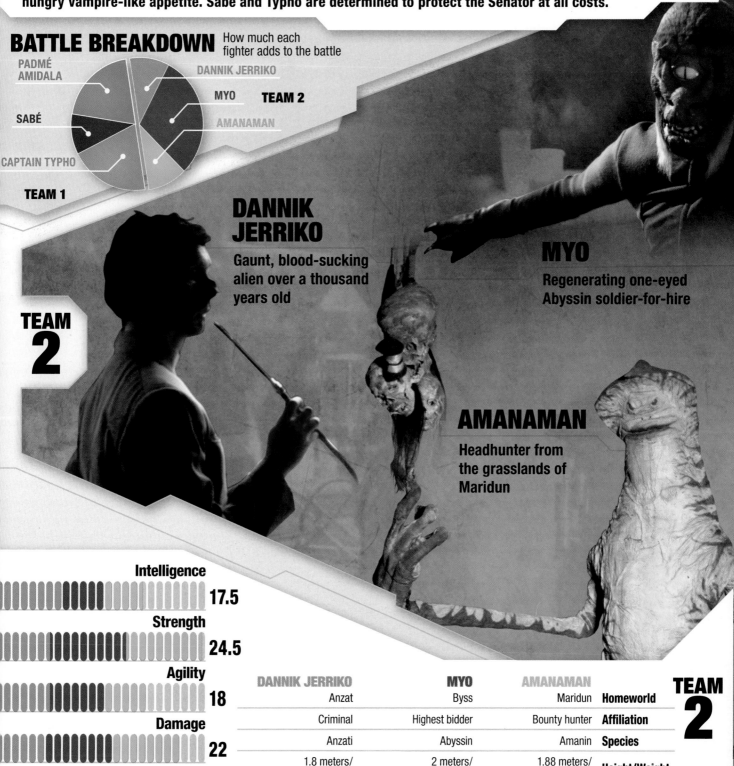

BATTLE BREAKDOWN
How much each fighter adds to the battle

PADMÉ AMIDALA
DANNIK JERRIKO
MYO   TEAM 2
SABÉ
AMANAMAN
CAPTAIN TYPHO
TEAM 1

TEAM 2

DANNIK JERRIKO
Gaunt, blood-sucking alien over a thousand years old

MYO
Regenerating one-eyed Abyssin soldier-for-hire

AMANAMAN
Headhunter from the grasslands of Maridun

	Intelligence	17.5
	Strength	24.5
	Agility	18
	Damage	22
	Control	20
	Courage	19

DANNIK JERRIKO	MYO	AMANAMAN		TEAM 2
Anzat	Byss	Maridun	**Homeworld**	
Criminal	Highest bidder	Bounty hunter	**Affiliation**	
Anzati	Abyssin	Amanin	**Species**	
1.8 meters/ 80 kilograms	2 meters/ 93 kilograms	1.88 meters/ 85 kilograms	**Height/Weight**	
Blaster pistol	Heavy blaster pistol	Blaster pistol, grenade, spear	**Weapons**	
Vampiric attack	Headlock	Rolling attack	**Special move**	

Who wins? See page 64.

There are endless questions to explore through the Force, such as, what if Jango Fett had survived to see his clones in action? He said to Obi-Wan that his genetic duplicates would do their job well, but what if the clones' assignment was to capture the bounty hunter known to associate with the leadership of the Separatist Alliance?

BATTLEGROUND

KAMINO: Tipoca City

JANGO FETT

Galaxy's top bounty hunter, template for the entire clone army

TEAM 1

YOUNG BOBA FETT

Unaltered clone of Jango Fett, raised as Jango's son

TEAM 1

	JANGO FETT	YOUNG BOBA FETT
Homeworld	Concord Dawn	Kamino
Affiliation	Bounty hunter	Bounty hunter
Species	Human	Human
Height/Weight	1.83 meters/ 79 kilograms	1.4 meters/ 37 kilograms
Weapons	Twin WESTAR-34 blaster pistols, rocket launcher, flamethrower, snare, rocket darts, climbing blades	DC-15A blaster pistol
Special move	Flamethrower attack	Stun blast

Intelligence
12

Strength
12.5

Agility
14

Damage
15

Control
15

Courage
18

THE SHOWDOWN

At first, Prime Minister Lama Su is hesitant to let the clone soldiers apprehend Jango, for the Kaminoan knows the monetary value of the original clone template. But Su also recognizes that loyalty to the Republic is better for business. Cody is reluctant to open fire on the clone host, but Bacara does not exhibit any such sentimentality. They both agree, however, to spare Boba unless the child actively threatens them—something Boba is determined to do if his father is in danger.

BATTLE BREAKDOWN

Genetic similarity to the original clone template

JANGO FETT

BOBA FETT

COMMANDER CODY

COMMANDER BACARA

LAMA SU

100% 100% 91% 84% N/A

COMMANDER BACARA

Fiercely independent, aggressive commander of the Galactic Marines

COMMANDER CODY

By-the-book officer, leader of Ghost Company and the 212th Attack Battalion

TEAM 2

LAMA SU

Political leader of the Kaminoan cloning operation

Intelligence **21.5**

Strength **18**

Agility **14**

Damage **17.5**

Control **20.5**

Courage **22**

	COMMANDER CODY	COMMANDER BACARA	LAMA SU	
	Kamino	Kamino	Kamino	**Homeworld**
	Galactic Republic	Galactic Republic	Galactic Republic	**Affiliation**
	Human clone	Human clone	Kaminoan	**Species**
	1.83 meters/ 80 kilograms	1.83 meters/ 80 kilograms	2.29 meters/ 88 kilograms	**Height/Weight**
	DC-15 blaster rifle, DC-15a blaster	DC-15 blaster rifle, DC-15a blaster	Hold-out stun blaster	**Weapons**
	Spin kick	Strangle attack	Vital organ strike	**Special move**

TEAM 2

Who wins? See page 64.

SHAAK TI, AAYLA SECURA & COMMANDER BLY VS. ZUCKUSS, BOSSK & WAMPA

Jedi Knights Shaak Ti and Aayla Secura, along with loyal clone officer Bly, follow scattered leads to the uncharted Hoth system, where they are led into a mercenary trap. Zuckuss and Bossk have hatched a plan to collect Jedi bounties by luring their prey into a wampa cave, so the aggravated snow beast might soften up their targets.

BATTLEGROUND
Hoth:
Lanteel Glacier

AAYLA SECURA
Acrobatic Jedi warrior

SHAAK TI
Togruta Jedi Master, member of the Jedi Council, and clone training supervisor

COMMANDER BLY
Dedicated soldier pledged to defend the Republic

TEAM 1

TEAM 1		SHAAK TI	AAYLA SECURA	COMMANDER BLY
	Homeworld	Shili	Ryloth	Kamino
	Affiliation	Jedi	Jedi	Galactic Republic
	Species	Togruta	Twi'lek	Human clone
	Height/Weight	1.78 meters/ 57 kilograms	1.72 meters/ 55 kilograms	1.83 meters/ 80 kilograms
	Weapons	Lightsaber (blue blade)	Lightsaber (blue blade)	DC-15 blaster, twin DC-17 hand blasters
	Special move	Disarming blow	Nexu-stance evasive roll	Running strafe

Intelligence 21.5
Strength 22.5
Agility 20.5
Damage 24
Control 25
Courage 28

THE SHOWDOWN

This diabolical trap came to Zuckuss in one of his fevered dreams, though the vision failed to detail just how unpredictable an aggravated wampa could be. The howling beast at first focuses his rage on the Jedi, but it has no loyalty to the hunters—it wants all the intruders out of its cave. The hunters must carefully protect themselves from the ice monster, while trying to keep the Jedi and Bly at bay.

BATTLE BREAKDOWN
How much each fighter adds to the battle

- SHAAK TI
- TEAM 1
- AAYLA SECURA
- COMMANDER BLY
- ZUCKUSS
- TEAM 2
- BOSSK
- WAMPA

ZUCKUSS
Bounty hunter with mystical tracking techniques

TEAM 2

BOSSK
Hulking reptilian bounty hunter with a deadly appetite

WAMPA
Mighty and solitary hunter native to the frozen wastes of Hoth

Intelligence 13

Strength 12 ▸ 28.5

Agility 13

Damage 22.5

Control 19

Courage 16

	ZUCKUSS	BOSSK	WAMPA		TEAM 2
Homeworld	Gand	Trandosha	Hoth		
Affiliation	Bounty hunter	Bounty hunter			
Species	Gand	Trandoshan			
Height/Weight	1.5 meters/ 70 kilograms	1.9 meters/ 113 kilograms	3 meters/ 150 kilograms		
Weapons	GRS-1 snare rifle	Blaster rifle, grenade launcher, flamethrower	Claws, fangs, horns		
Special move	Tangle strike	Raking claws	Face swat		

Who wins? See page 64.

ORRIMAARKO, MAJOR PANNO & TEEBO VS. MAJOR MARQUAND, LIEUTENANT WATTS & AT-ST WALKER

Among the soldiers of the Rebel strike force dispatched to the forest moon of Endor were highly trained Dressellian commandos, freedom fighters from an Imperial-occupied world. They fight with a ferocity born from watching their planet Dressel exploited by Imperial greed. On Endor they have their chance for payback—even if it is against a heavily armed Imperial scout walker.

BATTLEGROUND
Endor:
Forest moon

MAJOR PANNO
Shrewd tactician experienced in fighting against overwhelming enemy numbers

ORRIMAARKO
Famed resistance fighter

TEEBO
Inquisitive Ewok, shaman student

TEAM 1

	ORRIMAARKO	MAJOR PANNO	TEEBO
Homeworld	Dressel	Dressel	Forest moon of Endor
Affiliation	Rebel Alliance	Rebel Alliance	Rebel Alliance
Species	Dressellian	Dressellian	Ewok
Height/Weight	1.8 meters/ 80 kilograms	1.82 meters/ 80 kilograms	1.32 meters/ 50 kilograms
Weapons	Dressellian projectile rifle, heavy blaster pistol, knife, thermal detonator	Blaster rifle, stun grenade, vibroblade, thermal detonator	Stone hatchet
Special move	Knife-throw	Commando strike	Rock toss

Intelligence 19
Strength 20.5
Agility 17
Damage 19
Control 22.5
Courage 30 ◄10

Teebo acts as a lure for the scout walker, taunting the pilots with well-lobbed rocks that bounce harmlessly off the AT-ST's armored skin. The vehicle plods into a thick grove of trees concealing the Dressellians, who drop from above onto the walker's head. Teebo and the commandos do all they can to stay close to the AT-ST, where its weapons cannot target them, but this leaves them vulnerable to the walker's crushing feet. Marquand and Watts realize they may need to exit their protective cockpit to deal with their foes.

BATTLE BREAKDOWN
Comparative hand-to-hand combat skill

MAJOR PANNO
ORRIMAARKO
TEEBO
MAJOR MARQUAND
LIEUTENANT WATTS

LIEUTENANT WATTS
Academy-trained Imperial Army gunner

MAJOR MARQUAND
Academy-trained Imperial Army officer

TEAM 2

AT-ST WALKER
Lightweight Imperial walker designed for recon and support

Intelligence 14

Strength 30 ► 40.5

Agility 17

Damage 20 ► 30

Control 20

Courage 12

	MAJOR MARQUAND	LIEUTENANT WATTS	AT-ST WALKER	
Homeworld	Kessel	Corulag		
Affiliation	Galactic Empire	Galactic Empire	Galactic Empire	
Species	Human	Human	All Terrain Scout Transport	
Height/Weight	1.74 meters/ 75 kilograms	1.78 meters/ 70 kilograms	8.6 meters/ 12,100 kilograms	
Weapons	Blaster pistol	Blaster pistol	Twin blaster cannon, twin light blaster cannon, grenade launcher	
Special move	Throwback punch	Academy uppercut	Stomp attack	

TEAM 2

Who wins? See page 64.

DEXTER JETTSTER, DANNL FAYTONNI & ACHK MED-BEQ
VS.
ELAN SLEAZEBAGGANO & TONNIKA SISTERS

The shadowy streets of Coruscant can be treacherous, especially for those who try to avoid the glaring search beams of the law. Deep in the underworld, a trio who deals in selling information—a diner owner and two con men—follows a lead that turns sour, sparking an alleyway altercation that lights up the back streets with blaster fire.

BATTLEGROUND
Coruscant:
Entertainment District

DANNL FAYTONNI
Con man who has grown accustomed to his stolen officer's uniform

DEXTER JETTSTER
Crafty owner of Dex's Diner

TEAM 1

ACHK MED-BEQ
Inventive and ambitious con artist

TEAM 1

	DEXTER JETTSTER	DANNL FAYTONNI	ACHK MED-BEQ
Homeworld	Ojom	Corellia	Corellia
Affiliation	Friend to the Jedi	Criminal	Criminal
Species	Besalisk	Human	Human
Height/Weight	1.88 meters/ 102 kilograms	1.65 meters/ 71 kilograms	1.8 meters/ 78 kilograms
Weapons	Vibroblade	Hold-out blaster	Blaster pistol
Special move	Tenderizing quadruple punch	Nerve-cluster pinch	Double jab

Intelligence 22.5

Strength 19

Agility 16

Damage 15.5

Control 16

Courage 19

THE SHOWDOWN

Though on the surface Dexter seems the amiable sort, here in the shadows his hardened survival instincts turn him into an imposing opponent. His thick body is well muscled, and his con men partners stay in fighting shape. Years of hard living in the undercity have weakened Elan's health, but his blade edge is as sharp as ever. The sisters far prefer a scam or a heist to gunplay, but they will protect each other to the end.

BATTLE BREAKDOWN
Comparative combat experience

- DEXTER JETTSTER
- DANNL FAYTONNI
- ACHK MED-BEQ
- TONNIKA SISTERS
- ELAN SLEAZEBAGGANO

ELAN SLEAZEBAGGANO

Sordid thief and seller of illegal goods

TONNIKA SISTERS

Identical twins who use their charms to trick gullible men

TEAM 2

	ELAN SLEAZEBAGGANO	TONNIKA SISTERS	
Intelligence	Coruscant	Kiffex	**Homeworld**
12	Criminal	Criminal	**Affiliation**
Strength	Balosar	Kiffar	**Species**
10	1.78 meters/ 70 kilograms	1.6 meters/ 51 kilograms	**Height/Weight**
Agility	Vibroblade	Blaster pistol	**Weapons**
10	Deliberately clumsy and unpredictable fighting style	Back-to-back defensive parries	**Special move**
Damage			
11			
Control			
10.5			
Courage			
8			

TEAM 2

Who wins? See page 64.

RATTS TYERELL, MARS GUO & ALDAR BEEDO  VS. TEEMTO PAGALIES, BEN QUADINAROS & ODY MANDRELL

Podrace competitors are rarely examples of great sportsmanship, and this quarrelsome group has erupted into a pre-race dust-up. Insults about each other and their vehicles have sparked a brawl right at the starting line of the arena. Podracing is dangerous both on and off the course.

BATTLEGROUND
Tatooine:
Mos Espa Grand Arena

MARS GUO
Obnoxious pilot with a big ego

RATTS TYERELL
A scrappy little Aleena, Tyerell is tougher than his appearance suggests

ALDAR BEEDO
Secret hit man working for the highest bidder

TEAM 1

Intelligence
14.5

Strength
15

Agility
16.5

Damage
15

Control
17.5

Courage
20

TEAM 1

	RATTS TYERELL	MARS GUO	ALDAR BEEDO
Homeworld	Aleen	Phu	Ploo II
Affiliation	Professional Podrace circuit	Professional Podrace circuit	Bounty hunter
Species	Aleena	Phuii	Glymphid
Height/Weight	0.79 meters/ 15 kilograms	1.42 meters/ 35 kilograms	1.3 meters/ 32 kilograms
Weapons	Vibroblade	Blaster pistol	Hold-out blaster pistol, knife
Special move	Cranial fan head-butt	Peck	Concealed blaster gut-shot

As a hired gun, Aldar Beedo is the most experienced combatant, but he has to keep his true occupation secret. Though his large hands conceal a blaster, he's hesitant to use it, as none of the rowdy racers are his target. Teemto focuses on his rival Mars, while Ratts is eager to clobber anyone within his tiny reach. Ody finds the whole mess hilarious and dives into the thick of the brawl with a grin on his face. Ben, terrified of the noise, tries to slink away unnoticed. When the brawlers take to their vehicles, the fight becomes a chase.

BATTLE BREAKDOWN
Vehicle speeds

BEN QUADINAROS	940 kph (if it starts)
RATTS TYRELL	841 kph
ALDAR BEEDO	823 kph
MARS GUO	790 kph
TEEMTO PAGALIES	775 kph
ODY MANDRELL	750 kph

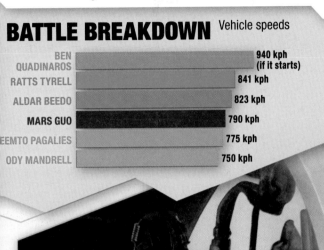

BEN QUADINAROS
Hopelessly inexperienced racer

TEAM 2

TEEMTO PAGALIES
Flamboyant and aggressive competitor on the track

ODY MANDRELL
Reckless thrill-seeker

Intelligence	16
Strength	13.5
Agility	15.5
Damage	11
Control	14
Courage	19.5

	TEEMTO PAGALIES	BEN QUADINAROS	ODY MANDRELL	
Homeworld	Moonus Mandel	Toong'l	Tatooine	**Homeworld**
Affiliation	Professional Podrace circuit	Professional Podrace circuit	Professional Podrace circuit	**Affiliation**
Species	Veknoid	Toong	Er'Kit	**Species**
Height/Weight	1.37 meters/ 55 kilograms	1.63 meters/ 65 kilograms	1.63 meters/ 58 kilograms	**Height/Weight**
Weapons	None	None	Blaster pistol	**Weapons**
Special move	Big squeeze	Frustrated pummeling	Head-first tackle	**Special move**

TEAM 2

Who wins? See page 64.

JEDI LUKE SKYWALKER, ADMIRAL ACKBAR & R2-D2 — VS. — WORRT, MYNOCK & DIANOGA

Investigating a seemingly derelict Imperial cruiser, Admiral Ackbar and Luke Skywalker wander into a dank chamber, following R2-D2's faint sensor readings of life-forms. Rather than survivors, they find scavenging creatures in a magnetically sealed garbage masher—that suddenly becomes active!

BATTLEGROUND
Imperial cruiser:
Trash compactor

ADMIRAL ACKBAR
Brilliant tactician and fleet officer

R2-D2
Trusty and versatile astromech droid

JEDI LUKE SKYWALKER
Rebel Alliance hero, destroyer of the Death Star, last of the Jedi

TEAM 1

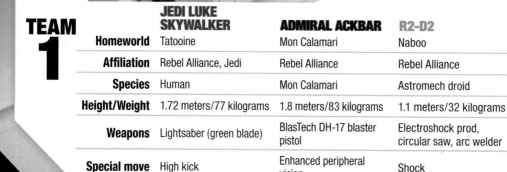

TEAM 1

	JEDI LUKE SKYWALKER	ADMIRAL ACKBAR	R2-D2
Homeworld	Tatooine	Mon Calamari	Naboo
Affiliation	Rebel Alliance, Jedi	Rebel Alliance	Rebel Alliance
Species	Human	Mon Calamari	Astromech droid
Height/Weight	1.72 meters/77 kilograms	1.8 meters/83 kilograms	1.1 meters/32 kilograms
Weapons	Lightsaber (green blade)	BlasTech DH-17 blaster pistol	Electroshock prod, circular saw, arc welder
Special move	High kick	Enhanced peripheral vision	Shock

Intelligence 20.5

Strength 18

Agility 16

Damage 16

Control 21

Courage 26

THE SHOWDOWN

The animals aren't the most deadly foes in the room: The room itself is a real problem! With every passing minute, the walls move closer to one another. As the space tightens, the scavengers become more frenzied and dangerous. The magnetic seal means Ackbar must be careful with his blaster, or a missed shot might become a deadly ricochet. The seal protects the door from Luke's lightsaber, but R2-D2 may have the tools he needs to bypass the lock if he's given time to work. Unfortunately, the Mynock sees the energy-rich R2-D2 as the tastiest target in the room. Meanwhile, the dianoga is looking for a victim to drag under the scummy water.

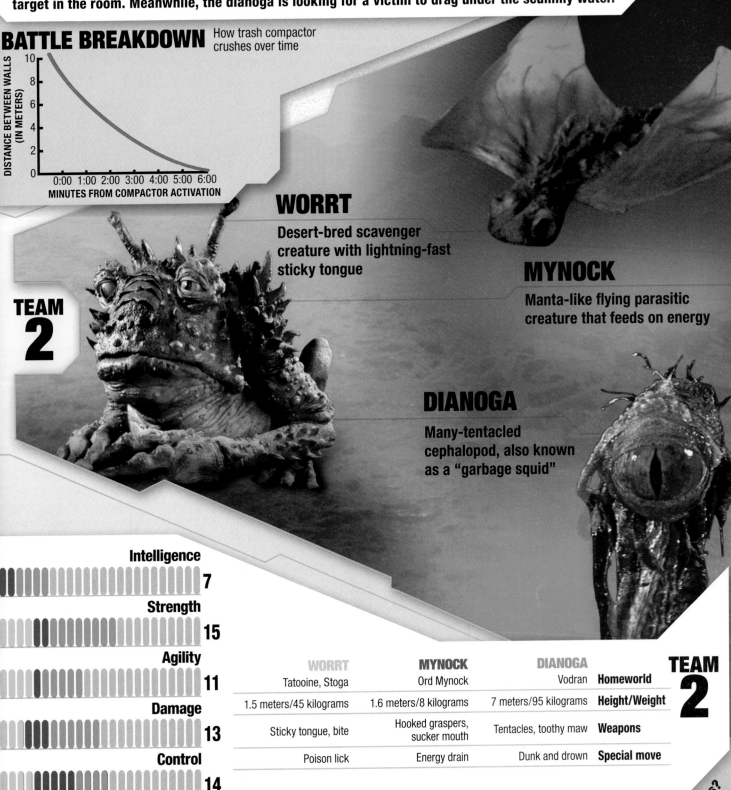

BATTLE BREAKDOWN How trash compactor crushes over time

(Graph: DISTANCE BETWEEN WALLS (IN METERS) vs. MINUTES FROM COMPACTOR ACTIVATION, x-axis from 0:00 to 6:00, y-axis from 0 to 10)

WORRT
Desert-bred scavenger creature with lightning-fast sticky tongue

MYNOCK
Manta-like flying parasitic creature that feeds on energy

DIANOGA
Many-tentacled cephalopod, also known as a "garbage squid"

TEAM 2

Intelligence **7**

Strength **15**

Agility **11**

Damage **13**

Control **14**

Courage **12**

	WORRT	MYNOCK	DIANOGA	
	Tatooine, Stoga	Ord Mynock	Vodran	**Homeworld**
	1.5 meters/45 kilograms	1.6 meters/8 kilograms	7 meters/95 kilograms	**Height/Weight**
	Sticky tongue, bite	Hooked graspers, sucker mouth	Tentacles, toothy maw	**Weapons**
	Poison lick	Energy drain	Dunk and drown	**Special move**

TEAM 2

Who wins? See page 64.

DOCTOR EVAZAN & PONDA BABA VS. & MUFTAK, KABE & MOMAW NADON

The grotesque Doctor Evazan has bragged about the death sentence on his head one too many times. Muftak and Kabe, a pair of Mos Eisley street urchins eager to make a few credits, attempt to cash in on the bounty. They assume Evazan is exaggerating about his reputation, but they may have underestimated the twisted doctor and his walrus-faced bodyguard, Ponda Baba.

BATTLEGROUND

Tatooine:
Mos Eisley:
Docking Bay 94

DOCTOR EVAZAN

Twisted doctor wanted in 12 systems for performing cruel experiments

PONDA BABA

Surly smuggler, pirate, and hired gun

TEAM 1

TEAM 1

	DOCTOR EVAZAN	PONDA BABA
Homeworld	Unknown	Ando
Affiliation	Criminal	Criminal
Species	Human	Aqualish
Height/Weight	1.7 meters/ 80 kilograms	1.85 meters/ 84 kilograms
Weapons	SE-14c blaster pistol	Chrome blaster pistol
Special move	Vital organ-targeted blast	Powerful right hook

Intelligence
13

Strength
14

Agility
11

Damage
14.5

Control
13

Courage
11.5

THE SHOWDOWN

"You just watch yourself!" crows a hot-tempered Doctor Evazan as Muftak looms threateningly close. Ponda Baba, protective of the insane doctor, rushes to defend him, but the Aqualish discovers his holster empty when he goes for the quick-draw: Kabe has pickpocketed his weapon. That leaves only Evazan with a gun, but Ponda is in the way, preventing him from getting a clear shot. Momaw Nadon watches for an opportunity to protect his friends, though he's reluctant to inflict any harm, no matter how deserving his foe.

BATTLE BREAKDOWN
Comparative combat experience

- PONDA BABA
- DOCTOR EVAZAN
- MUFTAK
- MOMAW NADON
- KABE

MUFTAK
Burly alien with a childlike side

TEAM 2

KABE
Expert pickpocket and master of escaping tight situations

MOMAW NADON
Peaceful, dependable gardener

Intelligence 19.5

Strength 19

Agility 17

Damage 15

Control 15

Courage 19.5

TEAM 2

MUFTAK	KABE	MOMAW NADON	
Alzoc III	Chad	Ithor	**Homeworld**
None	None	Rebel Alliance	**Affiliation**
Talz	Chadra-Fan	Ithorian	**Species**
2.1 meters/ 110 kilograms	0.96 meters/ 31 kilograms	1.95 meters/ 90 kilograms	**Height/Weight**
A beat-up blaster pistol	Vibroblade	Staff, blaster pistol	**Weapons**
Furry-knuckled uppercut	Ankle-bite	Rash-inducing plant powder throw	**Special move**

Who wins?
See page 64.

LUMINARA UNDULI & BARRISS OFFEE VS. POGGLE THE LESSER & REEK

During the Clone Wars, the Separatists retook Geonosis, requiring the Republic to return to that red-rock planet. Braving harsh desert storms and droid armies, Jedi Luminara and Barriss follow the fleeing Separatist leader Poggle the Lesser into one of his massive droid factories.

LUMINARA UNDULI

Agile and precise Jedi Master

BATTLEGROUND

Geonosis:
Droid factory

BARRISS OFFEE

Luminara's dedicated teenage Padawan

TEAM 1

TEAM 1		LUMINARA UNDULI	BARRISS OFFEE
	Homeworld	Mirial	Mirial
	Affiliation	Jedi	Jedi
	Species	Mirialan	Mirialan
	Height/Weight	1.7 meters/ 56.2 kilograms	1.66 meters/ 50 kilograms
	Weapons	Lightsaber (green blade)	Lightsaber (blue blade)
	Special move	Force push	Blunt pommel strike

Intelligence
13.5

Strength
10.5

Agility
15.5

Damage
14

Control
15

Courage
17

THE SHOWDOWN

Poggle's main objective is to escape, rather than defeat the Jedi, but he will fight if his pursuers give him no choice. The reek sticks to the open areas of the factory, which means the Jedi aren't led toward the clanking heavy machinery that surrounds them. Hoping to buy some time, Poggle releases the reek to charge the Jedi. Luminara focuses on the creature, while Barriss jumps overhead, determined to bring the Geonosian to justice. Poggle takes wing and flutters to one of the higher conveyer belts, but Barriss does not give up easily.

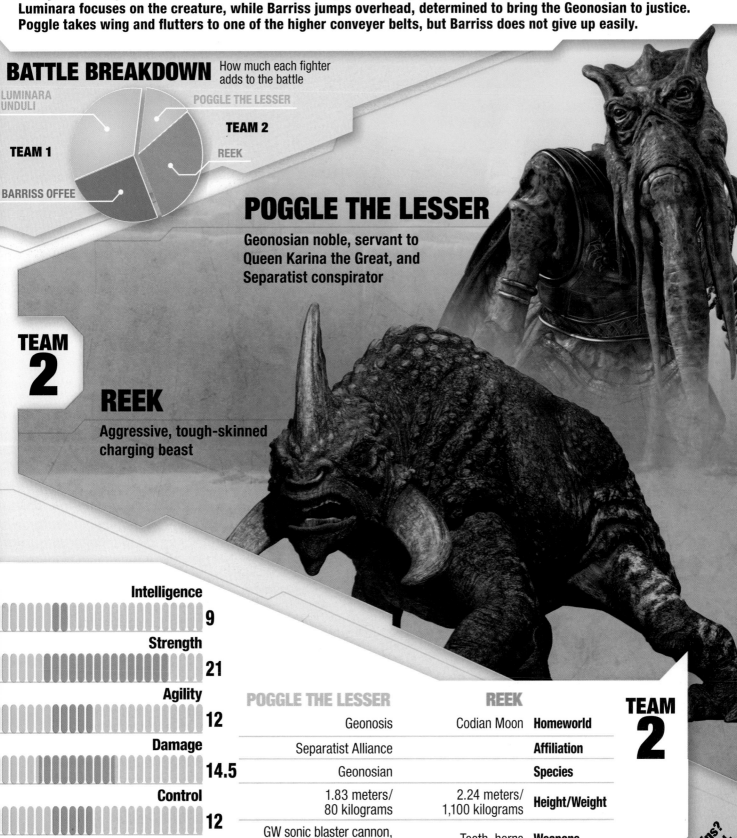

BATTLE BREAKDOWN
How much each fighter adds to the battle

LUMINARA UNDULI

POGGLE THE LESSER

TEAM 2

TEAM 1

REEK

BARRISS OFFEE

POGGLE THE LESSER

Geonosian noble, servant to Queen Karina the Great, and Separatist conspirator

TEAM 2

REEK

Aggressive, tough-skinned charging beast

Intelligence		9
Strength		21
Agility		12
Damage		14.5
Control		12
Courage		10

POGGLE THE LESSER	REEK	
Geonosis	Codian Moon	**Homeworld**
Separatist Alliance		**Affiliation**
Geonosian		**Species**
1.83 meters/ 80 kilograms	2.24 meters/ 1,100 kilograms	**Height/Weight**
GW sonic blaster cannon, electro-pike	Teeth, horns	**Weapons**
Dive-bomb attack	Bite	**Special move**

TEAM 2

Who wins? See page 64.

MAX REBO, DROOPY MCCOOL & SY SNOOTLES VS. FIGRIN D'AN, NALAN CHEEL & DOIKK NA'TS

No one ever said the hyperspace lane to stardom was easy to navigate. Musicians performing in the seedier spaceports of the Outer Rim Territories often face unreasonable dangers when trying to make a living. Jabba the Hutt has double-booked a lucrative gig—the wedding of one of his cousins. Rather than reward both bands, the wicked Hutt makes the musicians fight for their pay.

BATTLEGROUND
Tatooine:
Jabba's palace

DROOPY MCCOOL
Soft-spoken artist who often keeps to himself

MAX REBO
Elephantine keyboard player with a healthy appetite

TEAM 1

SY SNOOTLES
Powerful-voiced diva

TEAM 1		MAX REBO	DROOPY MCCOOL	SY SNOOTLES
	Homeworld	Orto	Kirdo III	Lowick
	Affiliation	Max Rebo Band	Max Rebo Band	Max Rebo Band
	Species	Ortolan	Kitonak	Pa'lowick
	Height/Weight	1.4 meters/ 80 kilograms	1.58 meters/ 82 kilograms	1.6 meters/ 48 kilograms
	Weapons	None	None	Hold-out blaster
	Special move	Floppy ear smack	Vicelike grip	Ear-piercing shriek

Intelligence 15.5

Strength 17

Agility 11

Damage 12

Control 14.5

Courage 17

The combatants are reluctant, but realize that the Hutt will likely kill them if they don't fight. Sy tries to rally Max with talk of a huge buffet after the fight, but she is at a loss when it comes to motivating Droopy. Figrin secretly bets on the outcome, favoring his band to win. Doikk and Nalan don't want to injure their hands. (Musicians can be very protective of their hands.) After much hesitation, the band members finally begin their brawl as Jabba chuckles at the ridiculous spectacle.

BATTLE BREAKDOWN
Musical instruments' effectiveness as weapons

- SY SNOOTLES (mic stand)
- FIGRIN D'AN (kloo horn)
- DOIKK N'ATS (fizzz)
- DROOPY MCCOOL (chidinkalu flute)
- NALAN CHEEL (bandfill)
- MAX REBO (red ball organ)

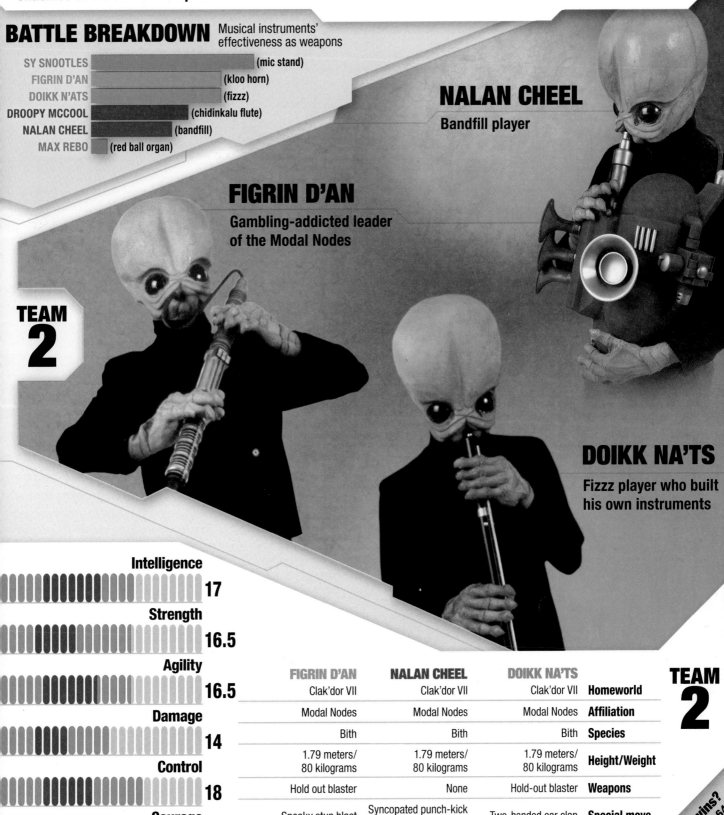

NALAN CHEEL
Bandfill player

FIGRIN D'AN
Gambling-addicted leader of the Modal Nodes

TEAM 2

DOIKK NA'TS
Fizzz player who built his own instruments

Intelligence **17**

Strength **16.5**

Agility **16.5**

Damage **14**

Control **18**

Courage **14.5**

	FIGRIN D'AN	NALAN CHEEL	DOIKK NA'TS	
	Clak'dor VII	Clak'dor VII	Clak'dor VII	**Homeworld**
	Modal Nodes	Modal Nodes	Modal Nodes	**Affiliation**
	Bith	Bith	Bith	**Species**
	1.79 meters/ 80 kilograms	1.79 meters/ 80 kilograms	1.79 meters/ 80 kilograms	**Height/Weight**
	Hold out blaster	None	Hold-out blaster	**Weapons**
	Sneaky stun blast	Syncopated punch-kick combo	Two-handed ear clap	**Special move**

TEAM 2

Who wins? See page 64.

2-1B & FX-7 VS. IT-0 & 8D8

Jawas aboard a massive sandcrawler are forcing their droid captives to fight for survival. Some of the more crafty tinkerers among the scavengers have modified a pair of medical droids to go on the offensive. Ordinarily, such droids could never comprehend harming another living being. Reprogramming these mechanical doctors to dismantle fellow droids, however, is well within the capability of a mischievous Jawa.

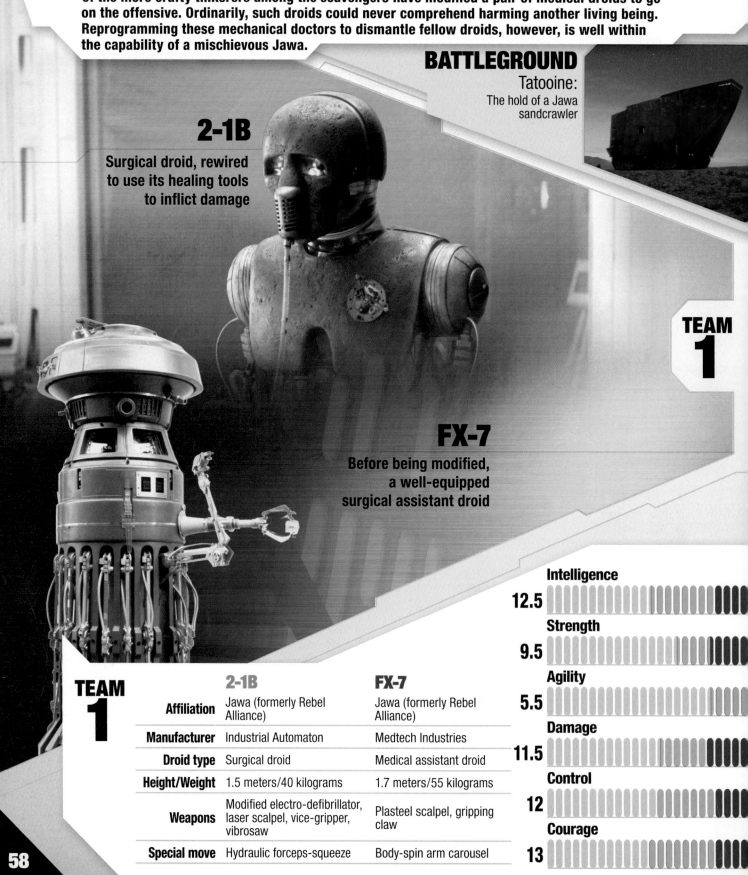

BATTLEGROUND
Tatooine: The hold of a Jawa sandcrawler

2-1B
Surgical droid, rewired to use its healing tools to inflict damage

FX-7
Before being modified, a well-equipped surgical assistant droid

TEAM 1

	2-1B	FX-7
Affiliation	Jawa (formerly Rebel Alliance)	Jawa (formerly Rebel Alliance)
Manufacturer	Industrial Automaton	Medtech Industries
Droid type	Surgical droid	Medical assistant droid
Height/Weight	1.5 meters/40 kilograms	1.7 meters/55 kilograms
Weapons	Modified electro-defibrillator, laser scalpel, vice-gripper, vibrosaw	Plasteel scalpel, gripping claw
Special move	Hydraulic forceps-squeeze	Body-spin arm carousel

Intelligence 12.5

Strength 9.5

Agility 5.5

Damage 11.5

Control 12

Courage 13

THE SHOWDOWN

At first, the medical droids are hesitant to take to their new programming, but upon sensor confirmation that their targets are not living organic beings, they raise their improvised weapons. They are used to operating as a team, analyzing each other's strengths, and compensating for the other's weaknesses. FX-7 is mostly stationary, apart from a set of rolling casters built into its base that allow it limited movement. IT-0 is programmed to be a solitary operator, and is an expert at devising new methods of destruction. 8D8 shares the same enthusiasm, but is nowhere near as imaginative.

BATTLE BREAKDOWN
Droid classifications and functions

DROID CLASSIFICATION	2-1B	FX-7	ITO	8D8
CLASS 1 (SCIENCES)	PRIMARY	PRIMARY	SECONDARY	
CLASS 2 (TECHNICAL)		SECONDARY	PRIMARY	PRIMARY
CLASS 3 (SOCIAL)	SECONDARY			
CLASS 4 (TACTICAL)				
CLASS 5 (MENIAL)				SECONDARY

IT-0
A terrifying example of Imperial engineering created for torturing Rebel prisoners

TEAM 2

8D8
Simply built smelter operator droid with an unmistakable mean streak

Intelligence 8

Strength 7.5

Agility 10

Damage 13.5

Control 8.5

Courage 8

	IT-0	8D8	
Affiliation	Jawa (formerly Galactic Empire)	Jawa (formerly criminal)	TEAM 2
Manufacturer	Imperial Dep. of Military Research	Roche	
Droid type	Interrogation droid	Smelter operator	
Height/Weight	0.3 meters/10 kilograms	1.83 meters/30 kilograms	
Weapons	Sonic torture device, electroshock assembly, grasping claw, laser scalpel, hypodermic injector syringe	Droid branding device	
Special move	Dive-bomb attack	Bite	

Who wins? See page 64.

GARINDAN, TION MEDON & SLY MOORE VS. WAT TAMBOR, LOTT DOD & LABRIA

Many times, crucial contests in the ongoing Clone Wars are decided by agents who work in the shadows, using deception and betrayal as their primary weapons. These administrators, officials, and spies are too valuable to be wasted in combat—but now, circumstances have forced them into the open.

BATTLEGROUND
Coruscant:
Galactic Senate chambers

TION MEDON
Ancient Utapaun administrator and secret resistance leader

GARINDAN
Long-snooted spy skilled at following his subjects undetected

SLY MOORE
Mysteriously silent agent of Chancellor Palpatine

TEAM 1

TEAM 1		GARINDAN	TION MEDON	SLY MOORE
	Homeworld	Kubindi	Utapau	Umbara
	Affiliation	Highest Bidder	Galactic Republic	Galactic Republic
	Species	Kubaz	Utapaun	Umbaran
	Height/Weight	1.85 meters/ 82 kilograms	2.06 meters/ 80 kilograms	1.78 meters/ 48 kilograms
	Weapons	Blaster pistol, hold-out blaster	Walking stick, blaster pistol	Hold-out blaster
	Special move	Shadow lurk	Long-reach backhand	Fear-inducing stare

Intelligence 24.5

Strength 16

Agility 19.5

Damage 13

Control 17

Courage 19

THE SHOWDOWN

Not seasoned warriors, these combatants nonetheless have all been plunged into do-or-die situations before, so they are prepared. Tion Medon instinctively takes a leadership position for his team, with Sly Moore using her powerful mental abilities to predict enemy attacks and distract their attentions. This works particularly well in combination with Garindan's stealth. Labria is the most martial of the opposing team, though he is out of practice. Lott scrambles into a floating Senate pod to gain extra height, while Wat uses a devastating prototype Techno Union weapon.

BATTLE BREAKDOWN
How much each fighter adds to the battle

GARINDAN
WAT TAMBOR
TEAM 2
LOTT DOD
TEAM 1
LABRIA
TION MEDON
SLY MOORE

LOTT DOD
Greedy Senatorial representative for the Trade Federation

WAT TAMBOR
Foreman of the Techno Union

TEAM 2

LABRIA
War criminal who adopted an alias while hiding from justice

	Intelligence				
	24.5				
	Strength 16				
	Agility 14.5				
	Damage 16.5				
	Control 15				
	Courage 12				

	WAT TAMBOR	LOTT DOD	LABRIA		
	Skako	Cato Neimoidia	Devaron	**Homeworld**	
	Techno Union	Trade Federation	None	**Affiliation**	
	Skakoan	Neimoidian	Devaronian	**Species**	
	1.93 meters/ 48 kilograms	1.9 meters/ 79 kilograms	1.8 meters/ 80 kilograms	**Height/Weight**	
	Prototype disruptor beam	Hold-out blaster, vial of poison	Hold-out blaster	**Weapons**	
	Disorienting sound distortion	Fake surrender	Horned head-butt	**Special move**	

TEAM 2

Who wins? See page 64.

DARTH MAUL & DARTH VADER  VS. QUI-GON JINN & YODA

A momentous battle erupts among the galaxy's most powerful warriors of the light side and dark side—an impossible conflict visible only to the most gifted of Jedi and Sith seers. Such are the mysteries of the Force that combatants separated by time and space—and even by death!—are able to cross lightsabers in an epic show of power!

BATTLEGROUND
Coruscant:
Jedi Temple

DARTH MAUL

Bold Sith warrior trained in the dark arts since childhood

TEAM 1

DARTH VADER

Fallen Jedi reborn as the half-mechanical Dark Lord of the Sith

TEAM 1

	DARTH MAUL	DARTH VADER
Homeworld	Dathomir	Tatooine
Affiliation	Sith	Sith, Galactic Empire
Species	Zabrak	Human
Height/Weight	1.75 meters/ 80 kilograms	2.02 meters/ 136 kilograms
Weapons	Double-bladed lightsaber (red blades)	Lightsaber (red blade)
Special move	Spin attack	Saber throw

Intelligence 13

Strength 20

Agility 12

Damage 14

Control 16

Courage 16

THE SHOWDOWN

Maul and Vader are experienced in carrying out the will of their Master, but being on a team is not their strength. Yoda and Qui-Gon are used to working with other Jedi, and their immediate defensive postures cover each other's weaknesses. Yoda's quick moves and nimble jumps complement Qui-Gon's long strides and reach. The impatient Maul leads the charge, creating a wide fan of deadly light when he swings his double lightsaber. Even Vader is forced to give him ample berth. Vader's steady, powerful strikes require full strength to parry and push back, but his mechanical body is clearly the slowest of the lot.

BATTLE BREAKDOWN
How much each fighter adds to the battle

DARTH MAUL

QUI-GON JINN

TEAM 2

TEAM 1

YODA

DARTH VADER

TEAM 2

QUI-GON JINN
Maverick Jedi Master who follows his own path

YODA
Wise Jedi Master who spent a generation in exile

Intelligence **16.5**

Strength **12**

Agility **16**

Damage **16**

Control **17.5**

Courage **20**

	QUI-GON JINN	YODA	
Homeworld	Unknown	Unknown	
Affiliation	Jedi	Jedi	
Species	Human	Unknown	
Height/Weight	1.93 meters/ 88.5 kilograms	0.66 meters/ 17 kilograms	
Weapons	Lightsaber (green blade)	Lightsaber (green blade)	
Special move	Force-assisted leap	Force push	

TEAM **2**

Who wins? See page 64.

THE EXPERTS' PICKS

p. 4–5:

Anakin Skywalker & Mace Windu vs. Count Dooku & Supreme Chancellor Palpatine

Winner: Team 2, Count Dooku & Supreme Chancellor Palpatine

Anakin fails to work effectively with Windu, and the Sith Lords triumph—though their plot is now exposed.

p. 6–7:

Luke Skywalker, Biggs Darklighter & Dewback vs. Gamorrean Guard, Giran & Jabba's Rancor

Winner: Team 2, Gamorrean Guard, Giran & Jabba's Rancor

The barely controllable rancor chomps Luke's dewback, but in its hurry to feed, it accidentally stomps on the Gamorrean. Luke and Biggs escape, leaving Giran to wait for his pet to finish feeding.

p. 8–9:

Sebulba, Dud Bolt & Pit Droid vs. Young Anakin, Kitster Banai & Wald

Winner: A draw

The pit droid becomes such a nuisance that it's all the combatants can do to tap it on the nose and deactivate it. The boys escape with a few bruises, but Sebulba and Dud get their power charge back.

p. 10–11:

Dengar & Greedo vs. Han Solo & Nien Nunb

Winner: Team 2, Han Solo & Nien Nunb

The smugglers work as a team. The bounty hunters trip over themselves as they both greedily target Han, which gives Nien the chance to tip the odds by taking out Greedo. Outclassed, Dengar retreats into the streets, letting Han and Nien escape.

p. 12–13:

Zam Wesell, Acklay & Nexu vs. Sun Fac, Varactyl & Orray

Winner: Team 1, Zam Wesell, Acklay & Nexu

Zam's sharpshooting takes care of Sun Fac's aerial advantage, while the nexu tears through the orray. Against those odds, the varactyl is soon overwhelmed.

p. 14–15:

Boba Fett & General Grievous vs. Obi-Wan Kenobi & Chewbacca

Winner: Team 2, Obi-Wan Kenobi & Chewbacca

Chewbacca is able to win against Grievous, leaving Obi-Wan the sole lightsaber combatant on the field. He and the Wookiee force Fett to retreat.

p. 16–17:

Nute Gunray, Rune Haako & Falumpaset vs. Jar Jar Binks, C-3PO & Sio Bibble

Winner: Team 2, Jar Jar Binks, C-3PO & Falumpaset

The Neimoidians are done in by their skittish mount, which bucks and tramples them.

p. 18–19:

General Veers, Imperial Royal Guard & Stormtrooper vs. MagnaGuard & IG-88

Winner: Team 2, MagnaGuard & IG-88

The battle is close, until IG-88 blasts out one of the room's viewports, blowing the air out into space, leaving only the droids standing.

p. 20–21:

Plo Koon, Ki-Adi-Mundi & Agen Kolar vs. Aiwha, Sando Aqua Monster & Colo Claw Fish

Winner: Team 1, Plo Koon, Ki-Adi-Mundi & Agen Kolar

As fierce and imposing as the sea beasts are, they have simple, singularly focused minds. Together, the Jedi are able to steer the sando back to its massive pen, though the colo dies of injuries and the aiwha simply flees.

p. 22–23:

Captain Tarpals & Kit Fisto vs. Mustafarian Thief & Lava Flea

Winner: Team 2, Mustafarian Thief & Lava Flea

The environment slows Kit and Tarpals down so much that the Mustafarian atop his flea is able to flee. He wins without even having to fight, escaping with the stolen goods.

p. 24–25:

Lando Calrissian, Cloud City Wing Guard & Lobot vs. Droideka & Ugnaughts

Winner: Team 1, Lando Calrissian, Cloud City Wing Guard & Lobot

Lobot is Lando's secret weapon. His connection to the computer network lets him limit the Ugnaughts' destructive potential.

p. 26–27:

Wedge Antilles & Jek Porkins vs. Captain Piett & TIE Fighter Pilot

Winner: Team 1, Wedge Antilles & Jek Porkins

Though they've won this fight, they've lost whatever objective the diplomatic meeting was trying to achieve.

p. 28–29:

Old Ben Kenobi & Ronto vs. Dice Ibegon, Lak Sivrak & Hem Dazon

Winner: Team 1, Old Ben Kenobi & Ronto

Kenobi mind-tricks his way through the scenario, though the ronto does not survive the encounter.

p. 30–31:

Merumeru & Tarfful vs. Tank Droid & Dwarf Spider Droid

Winner: Team 1, Merumeru & Tarfful

The Wookiees have the home-field advantage and are too agile for the heavy cannons of the droids to track.

p. 32–33:

Coleman Trebor & Adi Gallia vs. 4-LOM & Aurra Sing

Winner: Team 2, 4-LOM & Aurra Sing

It's close. 4-LOM doesn't survive, but provides support to let Aurra Sing defeat the Jedi, just as she planned.

p. 34–35:

Princess Leia & Wicket W. Warrick vs. A Dozen Buzz Droids

Winner: Team 1, Princess Leia & Wicket W. Warrick

Buzz droids are unsettling, but their weapons are designed to fight machinery that doesn't fight back.

p. 36–37:

Jabba the Hutt, Bubo & Pote Snitkin vs. Bantha, Tusken Chief & Tusken Raider

Winner: Team 2, Bantha, Tusken Chief & Tusken Raider

Let this be a lesson that the Jundland Wastes are not to be traveled lightly. They belong to the warlike Tuskens.

p. 38–39:

Padmé Amidala, Sabé & Captain Typho vs. Dannik Jerriko, Myo & Amanaman

Winner: Team 2, Dannik Jerriko, Myo & Amanaman

A costly battle: Only Dannik survives to claim his prize.

p. 40–41:

Jango Fett & Young Boba Fett vs. Commander Cody, Commander Bacara & Lama Su

Winner: Team 2, Commander Cody, Commander Bacara & Lama Su

The clones defeat Jango. Young Boba escapes—but he is now the clones' sworn enemy.

p. 42–43:

Shaak Ti, Aayla Secura & Commander Bly vs. Zuckuss, Bossk & Wampa

Winner: Team 1, Shaak Ti, Aayla Secura & Commander Bly

Though fierce, the wampa is not blaster- or lightsaber-proof.

p. 44–45:

Orrimaarko, Major Panno & Teebo vs. Major Marquand, Lieutenant Watts & AT-ST Walker

Winner: Team 1, Orrimaarko, Major Panno & Teebo

Well-placed explosives in the leg assembly cripple the AT-ST. Its outmatched pilots are forced to surrender.

p. 46–47:

Dexter Jettster, Dannl Faytonni & Achk Med-Beq vs. Tonnika Sisters & Elan Sleazebaggano

Winner: Team 1, Dexter Jettster, Dannl Faytonni & Achk Med-Beq

Dexter makes all the difference. Elan is overpowered and the sisters flee when the odds turn.

p. 48–49:

Ratts Tyerell, Mars Guo & Aldar Beedo vs. Teemto Pagalies, Ben Quadinaros & Ody Mandrell

Winner: Team 1, Ratts Tyerell, Mars Guo & Aldar Beedo

Despite Aldar's half-hearted efforts, Ratts's vigor tips the balance for his side.

p. 50–51:

Jedi Luke Sywalker, Admiral Akbar & R2-D2 vs. Worrt, Mynock & Dianoga

Winner: Team 1, Jedi Luke Sywalker, Admiral Akbar & R2-D2

Ackbar and Luke protect R2-D2 long enough for the droid to shut down the trash masher.

p. 52–53:

Doctor Evazan & Ponda Baba vs. Muftak, Kabe & Momaw Nadon

Winner: Team 2, Muftak, Kabe & Momaw Nadon

Muftak plows past Baba and knocks Evazan out cold. Before Baba can retaliate, Momaw douses the thug with a face full of rash power.

p. 54–55:

Luminara Unduli & Barriss Offee vs. Poggle the Lesser & Reek

Winner: Team 1, Luminara Unduli & Barriss Offee

A reek is no match for a lightsaber, and Luminara is soon able to join her Padawan in the chase for Poggle.

p. 56–57:

Max Rebo, Droopy McCool & Sy Snootles vs. Figrin D'an, Nalan Cheel & Doikk Na'ts

Winner: Team 1, Max Rebo, Droopy McCool & Sy Snootles

Everyone is shocked when Sy pulls out a blaster and the fight turns deadly. Who knew she'd had experience as an assassin?

p. 58–59:

2-1B & FX-7 vs. IT-O & 8D8

Winner: Team 1, 2-1B & FX-7

Surprisingly, the medical droids triumph. The Jawa programming proves effective, and the well-paired droids disrupt their opponents.

p. 60–61:

Garindan, Tion Medon & Sly Moore vs. Wat Tambor, Lott Dod & Labria

Winner: Team 2, Wat Tambor, Lott Dod, & Labria

Tambor's prototype weapon first takes out Sly, which dissolves her mental disruptions, returning the advantage to Labria's team.

p. 62–63:

Darth Maul & Darth Vader vs. Qui-Gon Jinn & Yoda

Winner: Team 2, Qui-Gon Jinn & Yoda

The Sith are undone by their inability to pool their powers, and the Jedi prevail.